ONE ON ONE

DON AKER

ONE ON ONE

HarperTrophyCanada™
An imprint of HarperCollinsPublishersLtd

Published by Harper*Trophy*Canada™, an imprint of HarperCollins Publishers Ltd

First Edition

HarperCollins books may be purchased for educational, business, or sales promotional use through our Special Markets Department.

HarperCollins Publishers Ltd
2 Bloor Street East, 20th Floor
Toronto, Ontario, Canada
M4W 1A8

www.harpercollins.ca

Library and Archives Canada Cataloguing in Publication

Aker, Don, 1955–
One on one / Don Aker. – 1st ed.

ISBN-13: 978-0-00-639531-7
ISBN-10: 0-00-639531-7

I. Title.

PS8551.K46O54 2005 jC813'.54 C2005-902063-6

HC 9 8 7 6 5 4 3 2 1

Printed and bound in the United States
Set in Dante

For my wife, who sees it all and shares it with me.

CHAPTER 1

"Yes!" Jared's fist pumped the air as the basketball swished through the old hoop over the garage door. He caught the ball on its first bounce, faked left, pivoted, and launched it into the crisp October air once more. The ball traced another perfect arc from his fingertips, up over the driveway, and down through the hoop again.

Arms raised in mock victory, Jared whistled and danced about, enacting the NBA championship moment he'd envisioned in his head a hundred times before. Fans leaped to their feet, their deafening cheers like trains roaring through the stadium. Sports commentators shouted into microphones as they played and then replayed the final seconds of the game, describing the precision of the winning shot and the phenomenon that was Jared St. George.

A blur of golden fur brought the eleven year old back to reality as Cal, Jared's yellow Lab, joined in the dance, his tail wagging fiercely as he barked and bounced along with the boy. Flushed from the exertion, Jared ran the back of his arm across his forehead to catch the droplets of sweat, then stooped to scruffle Cal's ears. The crinkle of paper in his jeans pocket wiped the mile-wide grin from his face.

"Aww, jeez," he said. He straightened, his adrenalin rush evaporating as he recalled what was written on the paper. He'd tried all afternoon not to think about it, focusing instead on the basketball tryouts that his best friend, Steve Lewis, had told him were being held next week. That news and shooting baskets had helped—at least for a little while. He checked his watch and saw he still had a couple of hours before his mother got home and he'd have to show her the letter. He shrugged. No sense wasting a perfectly good Friday afternoon worrying about how she was going to react. He pretty much knew, anyway.

Retrieving the ball, he spun it a few times on his index finger, then dribbled it back and forth between his legs, conjuring up the roar of the crowds once more. "He fakes a pass to the wing," he murmured, "then drives toward the basket." Jared took two hard steps forward and leaped into the air.

But before he could complete the shot, two sets of fingers raked his sides, tickling him.

"Hey!" Jared yelped as he stumbled away from the ball. "No fair!"

"Yes, fair!" his mother cried. Laughing, she deked around him and sprang toward the basket, but he'd managed to regain his footing and easily blocked her shot. The ball bounced harmlessly off the rim and disappeared into the hedge beside the garage.

"And the crowd goes wild!" Jared shouted as he strutted around his mother, his arms raised in triumph once more. Cal barked and pranced along beside him.

Terri St. George laughed. "Okay, Sure-Shot, enough already with the cheering. You win. Height advantage."

She shook her head and, like so many times in the past few months, Jared knew his mother was marvelling at how much he had grown. As he turned toward the hedge to retrieve the ball, he was a little surprised himself that the tops of the shrubs were now at eye level. He'd undergone a dramatic growth spurt since the beginning of summer, which had resulted in more than one trip to Value Village to find clothes that fit him. Besides filling out, he was now a couple of centimetres taller than his mother, something he delighted in reminding her whenever he got the chance.

"How come you're home already?" Jared asked as he

emerged from the hedge with the basketball under his arm. "I thought your shift didn't end till seven." He paced off the foul-shot distance from the hoop and raised the ball, readying himself for the throw.

His mother stepped in front of him and put her hands on the basketball. Reluctantly, he allowed her to take it. "I got Jerry to come in early for me," she said. "Thought it might be nice to eat supper together." She tossed the ball onto the lawn and put her arm around her son's shoulders, leading him and Cal toward the back door of their blue bungalow. "I was beginning to forget what you looked like."

He shot furtive glances toward the street. "Aww, Mom," he said, pulling away from her, "someone might see."

"See what? Me hugging my only kid? Is that a crime?" She sighed and pulled away from him, but not before running her hand over his head. "I still miss your hair," she said.

Jared grinned at her. He and Steve had decided in July to shave their heads, and their mothers had nearly burst blood vessels when they saw what the boys had done. It was Steve's dad who had put everything into perspective. "It's just hair," he'd said, grinning at their naked white scalps. "It'll grow back." But it was a slow process. Even now, three months later, his curly blond hair was barely long enough to muss.

Not that less hair had reduced the attention Jared got from girls he saw on the street or at the mall. During those rare times when his mother wasn't working and could coax him into helping her with the grocery shopping, she often teased him about the appreciative looks he got from girls his age and even older. Strangers smiled shyly, while girls from Cornwallis Middle School, where Jared was in grade six, greeted him by name. He always smiled back, but he'd keep walking, uncomfortable with all the attention.

Steve, in grade seven and much more worldly, kidded him about it and told Jared he'd gladly give up his favourite food—tacos—for even half that attention. Although he was shorter than Jared, Steve's square features and broadening shoulders attracted quite a few glances of their own, but he joked, "Most of them are just ricochets. Their eyes bounce off you and hit me."

People often remarked that Jared got his good looks from his mother. Long, auburn hair framed a face pretty enough for billboards or shampoo bottles, and her slim figure gave no hint of the Pepsi and chocolate bars she snacked on regularly. A fast metabolism, nervous energy, and her work as a nurse at the city's largest hospital kept her from putting on weight. Jared had his own share of fun teasing his mother about the men who turned and stared at her in checkout lines or at bus stops, but she'd elbow him in the ribs and tell him again how one guy in her life was more than enough, thank you very much. Jared's dad had left them both seven years ago, and she just didn't have much use for men at this point in her life.

There was one girl from Cornwallis Middle School who seemed to feel the same way about Jared. One time when he and his mom were at the mall, Jared bumped into a girl coming out the exit, her eyes focused on a book in her hand. When she glanced up at Jared, recognition reflected in her face, but she hurried by without saying a word. "That's Ellie," Jared had told his mother when she'd asked who the girl was. "She's in my class. Doesn't like me much." But Jared wasn't concerned one way or the other with the attention he got from his female classmates. His first love was basketball.

Which was why he was so anxious to share Steve's news now. "Guess what?" he said, opening the door and following his mother and Cal inside the bungalow. "Tryouts start next week!"

"Tryouts for what?"

"For the Cougars!" he exclaimed incredulously, then noticed his mother's teasing smile. He had talked of little else for the last three weeks. "Steve told me Coach Jamieson posted the notice today. Tryouts start next Thursday."

"Think you're ready?" she asked, hanging her sweater on the hook behind the door, then taking down a package of angel hair pasta from the cupboard above the stove. She pulled a pot from a drawer and handed it to him, and he began filling it with water while she took green and red peppers, tomatoes and mushrooms from the crisper of their old Kenmore refrigerator and laid them on the cutting board.

"I dunno. I *think* so, but Jamieson don't like to—"

"*Doesn't* like to," she corrected as she began slicing the vegetables.

Jared scowled. "He *doesn't* like to take on grade sixes. Only grade eights and maybe a few sevens make his team. Hardly ever grade sixes." He turned off the tap and put the pot of water on the stove to heat.

"I think I remember you telling me something like that," his mother said elaborately, and Jared knew she was teasing him again. He had announced that sad truth nearly every day since school had started seven weeks ago.

Cornwallis Middle School had a policy that all students take part in at least one extracurricular activity each year. Jared was already playing on the school's soccer team—which was finishing up an excellent season, thanks largely to his and Steve's offensive skills—so he had already fulfilled his extracurricular requirement for the year. A natural athlete, Jared would have tried out for soccer even without the school's policy. Yet, as much as he enjoyed soccer, it was Jamieson's Cougars that he most wanted to play for.

Coach Jamieson did not train losing teams. In fact, he had coached the Cornwallis Cougars to division championship status six years in a row. Jamieson was an okay grade eight science teacher, but his reputation as a basketball coach was almost legendary in the city. Kids who dreamed of becoming Cougars began training long before they walked through the doors of Cornwallis Middle School. Most, like Jared and Steve, played at the Y and joined community leagues. A few who had the money, like Jared's classmate Rafe Wells, paid for private coaching and spent summers at expensive basketball camps in the States. Everyone, however, was equal in Jamieson's eyes—he didn't give two hoots about your background. What counted was what you could do on the court during tryouts. Above all else, Coach Jamieson wanted to win.

And above all else, Jared St. George wanted to play.

Which was why he'd decided he wasn't going to show his mother the letter folded neatly out of sight in his pocket.

CHAPTER 2

Cal lay in the middle of the kitchen floor, splayed in the Saturday morning sunshine that filtered through the window over the sink. Suddenly, the dog's ears flicked forward and he huffed twice, and Jared waited for the back door to burst open. Sure enough, two seconds later it did.

"What'd she say?" Steve demanded as he entered the kitchen, letting the door slam shut behind him. He never knocked. He'd barged into the St. Georges' house almost daily since Jared and his mother had moved next door three years earlier. Jared's mother had once playfully asked him if he knew how to knock, but her humour was wasted on him. Steve Lewis was one of those people who thought social graces were things you said on Sunday at the supper table.

"Shhh!" Jared urged, glancing over his shoulder to see if his mother was within earshot. He pushed away his half-eaten bowl of Cheerios and got up from the table. Dumping the soggy remains into the compost container, he mumbled, "I didn't give it to her."

"Whaddya mean?" Steve demanded, his voice now an exaggerated whisper. "How could you *not* give it to her?"

Jared's mother had eaten breakfast earlier and was now getting ready for work, so Jared put his dishes, along with his mother's, into the sink, squirted the bargain-basement dish soap over them, and turned on the hot water. As he usually did while he waited for the sink to fill, he longed for a dishwasher like all his friends had. "I just didn't," he muttered.

Steve whistled under his breath. "Keaton's gonna call her if she don't get back to him."

Jared grimaced. "I know that," he said, quickly washing the dishes and leaving them on the dish rack to dry. "I'll just hafta make sure I answer the phone before she does." In fact, he'd watched his favourite program on the Discovery Channel last night with the cordless beside him on the sofa the whole time. Just in case.

"Before she does what?" his mother asked as she entered the kitchen, gathering her hair into a neat ponytail and tying it. She was wearing her nurse's uniform.

Jared gulped. "Um . . . uh . . ."

"Lookin' good, Mrs. S.," Steve said.

Jared knew his friend had made the remark to change the subject, but it wasn't an empty compliment.

"Why, thank you, Steve. And to what do we owe the pleasure of your company this morning?"

"Just collectin' the kid so we can go shoot some hoops," Steve replied. Although a year older than Jared, he actually looked younger beside his taller friend, so he seized every opportunity to remind everyone of the difference in their ages.

Jared's mom sighed. "Somehow I didn't *think* you two were heading to the library." After making sure her keys were in her purse, she glanced at the clock on the wall and frowned. "I hope that bus isn't early again." She turned to Jared. "I know you'll be in the park all morning, so I've left lunch money on your bureau."

"Thanks, Mom."

Jared's mother grabbed her sweater from the hook behind the door and pulled it on. "Kathy's baby has croup, so I'm covering part of her shift till her husband gets home. You'll be on your own for supper, okay? There's some pasta left over from last night—"

"I'm okay," Jared said.

"I left the number on the counter in case you need me—"

"I know the number."

"Steve's mother said you can stay over there till I get home—"

"Mom!"

Jared's mother sighed. "I know, I know—you can take care of yourself." She looked at him and smiled. "When did you get to be so grown up?" she asked softly.

Jared shrugged. "You're gonna miss your bus," he warned before she could get all mushy on him.

His mother looked at the clock again. "Yikes, you're right. Gotta go. You take care of my guy, okay, Steve?"

"Will do, Mrs. S.," Steve replied.

She planted a quick kiss on her son's forehead before dashing out the door. The two boys watched from the step as she hurried down the sidewalk toward the bus stop. Before she rounded the corner, she looked back and called something over her shoulder. Jared waved at her.

"What'd she say?" Steve asked.

"Math. Told me to spend some time on my math."

"Oh, man, you are so screwed," Steve said, clapping his friend on the back.

"I know," Jared muttered. "I know."

* * *

"Jeez, Cal!" Steve exclaimed. "That was *huge!*"

Jared looked up as he finished scooping the dog's poop into the plastic bag, his face burning. "Don't encourage him," he said. In fact, the dog actually seemed to be grinning at them. "Just once I wish he'd wait till we got home." Jared glanced around for a garbage can, saw one beside a park bench near the fountain, and jogged over to drop the bag into it. When he returned, his friend resumed his prepare-for-the-worst speech.

"Look, Jared, I had Keaton last year. He ain't one 'a those teachers who lets things slide. If your mom don't call him soon, he'll just end up on your doorstep."

Jared took Cal's leash from Steve and they headed out of the park. They had joined a basketball game in the park that morning and played hard till noon, Jared letting his worries drain away as he dribbled down the court and drove toward the basket again and again. Although the other players were a year or two older than the two friends, Jared and Steve had more than held their own, high-fiving each other whenever they made a play that allowed their team to score. Cal watched intently from the sidelines, barking noisily at every shot.

Both boys were trying out for the Cougars the following week, and they'd have lots of competition, since Cornwallis was one of the biggest middle schools in the city. Jared thought about some of the guys who were likely to try out for the team. Rafe Wells, for one. Although he was in the sixth grade with Jared, Rafe had an edge that Jared did not. Besides the fancy basketball camps he went to each summer and the private coaching he got all year round, his dad, Skylar Wells, was a city alderman who was running for mayor. More to the point, Wells owned The Digital Highway, an upscale computer store downtown, and he'd donated thirty-five computers to Cornwallis Middle School the previous week. As fair as everyone claimed Jamieson was, it would be tough, Jared thought, for the coach to overlook Rafe Wells when he showed up for tryouts.

Steve, though, stood an excellent chance of making the team—because of his skill, not some dumb computers. Steve had tried out for the Cougars when he was in grade six and hadn't made it, but he'd grown and improved a lot in the past year. Although still a little shorter than most guys his age, Steve was lightning-quick on powerful legs and could handle the ball better than some of the high school students they'd played against in past pick-up games. And he never gave up, even when the opposing team had double the points on the board. Give Steve the ball anywhere on the court, and he could get it to the hoop nearly every time.

Which made the two of them such a good team. Besides having the extra height and seemingly endless stamina, Jared's keen sense of distance and direction helped him sink almost every one of his shots, even from behind the three-point line. Together, the two of them were a force to be reckoned with.

But there was one big reason why Jared knew he probably wouldn't make the team. It wasn't because he was in grade six—that wasn't as big a problem as he sometimes imagined it to be. Although Jamieson rarely chose sixth-graders, there were two such students who had made the cut in the last four years, guys whose height and skill level were similar to Jared's. No, the real reason he probably wouldn't make it was his failing math mark. Mr. Keaton, Jared's teacher, never let sports interfere with his students' schoolwork, and Jamieson never accepted a player he might lose later because of academic probation. Athletes put on academic probation could not play sports until their marks improved. Jared had heard that the coach and Keaton had gone nose to nose over one player the year before last, and Jamieson had had to pull the kid off the team the week before the championships. He wouldn't let that happen again.

"Can we talk about somethin' else?" Jared sighed. The way he saw it, he still had the rest of the weekend to figure things out. No point ruining a Saturday worrying about things he couldn't control. Like math. He'd first had problems with that subject in third grade, when Mrs. Carvery had introduced Jared's class to times tables. It had been downhill for him ever since. Knowing his math facts was one thing. Understanding how to use them to solve problems was an entirely different matter. All those signs and symbols and operations seemed to be just waiting to trip him up. For him, math might as well have been Mandarin Chinese.

Despite the cool October breeze, both boys were still sweating from the game. "Let's stop at the deli for lunch," Steve suggested as they crossed the street.

Jared brightened. One surefire way to forget a problem was to create one for someone else. And who better than Ellie Brejovic, who was likely to be at her dad's deli. Where else would you be when you had no life?

CHAPTER 3

The sign outside read "Brejovic's Deli," but all Jared ever heard anyone call it was "Ellie's Deli" because the owner's daughter was a regular fixture there. Her dad was always bragging about her to his customers: *Ellie this* and *Ellie that*. He'd homeschooled her for several years, so she'd spent most of every workday at one of the back tables, reading books or doing homework. She began attending public school only last year, when she and Jared had been in the same grade five class at Wedgewood Elementary. And this year they were both in Mr. Keaton's grade six class. One of the smartest kids at both schools, Ellie Brejovic always had a book in her hand, even on the playground. She never took part in any of the games, never walked around the school chatting with other girls her own age, never did anything but read, read, read. The kind of weirdo who'd *live* in a library if she could.

And just the kind of weirdo that people liked to get a rise out of.

Jared wasn't the sort of person who gave other kids a hard time. His mother's motto had always been "live and let live," and Jared felt pretty much the same way. Over the years, he'd never gotten involved in the teasing and taunting that his classmates sometimes got caught up in. More often than not, he'd try to defuse the situation when he saw a student being bullied by others—which was probably the reason most people at Cornwallis, teachers included, liked him.

But Ellie Brejovic was different. There was just something about her that got under his skin, made him look the other way when classmates started in on her. They mocked her with names like "Ellie Belly" and "Smelly Ellie," although she wasn't overweight or underwashed. In fact, Ellie was slim and nearly as tall as Jared, and her long dark hair and even features would have been considered attractive on someone else. That is, someone who actually talked to people and didn't bury her head in a book all day. The nicknames were just unfortunate rhymes that some budding poet had invented, names that everyone knew embarrassed her. She tried not to show it, but Jared saw the red flush rise from her neck to her cheeks every time and knew her tormentors had scored a direct hit.

It wasn't that the girl queened it over everyone. Yeah, she knew the answers to all the teachers' questions. Yeah, she made the highest mark on practically every single test. And yeah, she'd even won the regional library's annual award three years in a row for most books read by an elementary student. But she never mentioned it to anyone, never tried to make people feel like they weren't as smart as she was. The problem, of course, was that she never said much of *anything* to anyone. Except maybe Felicity Flowers, a toad-like girl with stringy hair whose name seemed like a cruel joke. Usually, though, Ellie was off by herself with a book. Which, Jared guessed, could give people the idea she didn't like their company, maybe even thought she was better than them. Whatever the reason, when you'd failed every math quiz since the beginning of September and you were hiding a letter from your teacher that probably ruined any chance you might have to play for the Cougars, the thought of being able to unload some of that misery onto someone else was appealing.

At the beginning of the school year, Jared had wondered how Ellie was going to handle Cornwallis Middle School's extracurricular requirement. She'd proven to everyone time after time in gym class that she wasn't much of an athlete. But, of course, there were other things besides sports teams she could join—student government, the school newspaper, the drama club, the chess club, the debating club, the environmental club that took care of the school's recycling program, or any of a dozen other groups. The only problem was that she'd have to spend time with people in whatever group she joined, which was one thing Ellie *wasn't* good at.

Jared shook his head. He was sure Ellie was shuddering at the thought of joining a group, yet here he was, willing to give just about anything to get a spot on Jamieson's team. Of course, after reading what Mr. Keaton had written to his mother, he knew there was little chance of that happening, no matter *what* miracle he might hope for.

Tying Cal to a bench outside the deli, Jared felt his resentment toward the teacher begin to churn inside him, felt it work itself from irritation into annoyance and then into something else altogether. Looking up at the deli's sign, Jared thought of Ellie, who was probably inside. He smiled.

* * *

"What are you wanting, gentlemen?" Milo Brejovic asked in a booming voice. He had immigrated from Bosnia when Ellie was just a baby, but his accent was still thick and his use of the English language often resulted in some weird expressions. He was a tall, burly man with hairy forearms and hands the size of baseball mitts. New customers were always surprised when those huge hands whipped up delicious sandwiches in seconds, fingers flying nimbly from one bowl of ingredients to another.

Steve ordered a ham and cheese on rye and a Coke, while Jared asked for his favourite: turkey breast with lots of mustard and a Propeller root beer. In moments their order was ready, and they settled down to eat at a table near the window in the small L-shaped dining area. Jared was disappointed not to see Ellie anywhere.

"So, the way I see it," Steve said, "the only thing you can do is act like you *lost* the letter."

Jared rolled his eyes. Back to the letter again. He wished he'd never mentioned it to Steve. But that would have been next to impossible. They were so close that his mother even commented on how they sometimes finished each other's sentences. She'd once said he and Steve were more like brothers than friends. Probably *better* than brothers, Jared thought, since his mom had been fighting with her own brother for years, and the two hardly ever saw each other except for a few hours on Christmas Day. Which was just about as long as either of them could stand to be around each other before one of them made a remark that would set things off.

Steve was well into a long, involved explanation of how Jared might be able to "lose" the letter without too much backlash from either his mother or Mr. Keaton when Jared spied Ellie. She was sitting at a table near the back, eating a sandwich. A young couple with a baby carriage had been sitting at the table in front of her, blocking her from Jared's view, but now the couple was getting up to leave. Ellie was by herself. And reading a book, as usual.

Jared instantly felt a surge of irritation. It was as if the girl had deliberately held up a sign with the words "I'm with Stupid" and an arrow pointing directly at him.

Jared put down his sandwich and leaned back in his chair. He sniffed long and noisily, then cleared his throat. "You *smell* anything, Steve?" he asked.

Interrupted in the middle of devising his *Mission Impossible* letter-losing scheme, Steve gaped at him. "Huh?"

"Just wonderin' if you found the deli *smelly* today." Jared cocked his head to the left.

Steve glanced toward the back of the room and saw Ellie. She was looking at her book, but her eyes weren't moving now, just staring at the same spot on the page. Her cheeks were pink. Steve looked at Jared and frowned. "No, I don't."

Jared knew what his friend was thinking. Steve never took part in geek-bashing. "Losers got enough troubles without me addin' to 'em," he often said.

But Jared couldn't let it go. He thought about the fractions test he'd written on Thursday, the one he'd gotten back on Friday, the one he'd made twenty-seven percent on, the one that had resulted in Keaton writing that letter. The test Ellie had scored a perfect mark on. "You know what they say about a *smelly* deli," he commented, his words slicing the air.

Steve shrugged. "What?"

"Smelly delis can upset bellies." Jared hooted, but his laughter was humourless and sounded harsh in the little eatery. He glanced toward the front of the deli, where Mr. Brejovic was making sandwiches for three customers. If the man had heard him, he didn't let on. Jared turned again to look at Ellie.

She was gone.

CHAPTER 4

"So. Just *when* were you planning on showing this to me?" Jared's mother said from the top of the basement stairs. "Or *were* you?" She had his jeans in one hand and Mr. Keaton's letter in the other.

Jared's spoonful of Cheerios froze midway between the bowl and his mouth. He still hadn't made up his mind what to do with the letter, so he'd left it in the pocket of his jeans. Which he'd left on the floor of his room on Friday afternoon. And, as she did every Monday morning, his mother was doing laundry. She must have scooped up his dirty clothes while he was asleep. The image of an "I'm with Stupid" sign popped into his head again. He certainly deserved to have it pointing directly at him right now.

He put the spoon down. "Uh," he began, "I was *gonna*

show it to you . . ." Jared trailed off. There wasn't much point in making things worse by lying. "No," he said. "I wasn't."

His mother shook her head sadly. "What were you hoping would *happen,* Jared? Did you think that Mr. Keaton would forget all about it over the weekend? After writing *this?*" She smoothed out the letter. "If Jared's performance in math doesn't improve dramatically, he could very well lose the year," she read, then looked at her son and sighed. "Here it is the middle of October and *already* your teacher is talking about the possibility of your failing grade six."

"You know about me and math, Mom—"

"Yes, Jared, I know about you and math. God knows you've had enough trouble with it over the years. And I certainly haven't been able to help you with the new curriculum they're teaching, which is why I spent that money on a tutor last year. I never regretted working the extra shifts to pay for it, because I thought it was something you needed." She shrugged. "Even then you barely got through." She sat down beside him. "But you promised me that things would be different this year, that you'd get extra help at noon and after school, that you'd really buckle down with your homework. You *were* staying after school, weren't you? What were you doing when you didn't have soccer?"

Jared looked down at the bowl, feeling like the shape of each Cheerio: a great big zero. "Me and Steve—"

"Let me guess," his mother interrupted. "Playing basketball, right?"

Jared nodded.

"Well," she said, shaking her head sadly, "the chickens have come home to roost."

Jared had no idea what chickens had to do with anything, but he was pretty sure his goose was cooked.

* * *

"I . . . ah . . . I'm really glad you came," Mr. Keaton said as he held out his hand to Jared's mother. "I . . . uh . . . always find a face-to-face meeting more . . . ah . . . more helpful than a . . . than a telephone call."

Jared stared at the teacher, who was red in the face and stumbling over his words. Usually he was as cool as ice.

Jared's mom shook Mr. Keaton's hand firmly. "Thanks again for your letter. And I appreciate your seeing me on such short notice." She was referring, of course, to the call she had placed to the school that morning.

"Please," said the teacher, "have a seat." He directed her to a desk beside Jared. She slid into it while the teacher stood—seemingly frozen—for an awkward moment, then sat down in a seat across from her.

Jared looked away. He had been dreading this moment all day. Language arts, science, and social studies were a blur, and he hadn't even tried to pay attention in math. What was the point? *I'm with Stupid.* Yeah, they certainly were.

The teacher straightened his tie and opened a folder containing examples of Jared's math work. Handing them to Jared's mother, he said, "You'll see . . . ah . . . you'll see that Jared's problems don't . . . uh . . . they don't just involve computation errors."

Jared looked at Mr. Keaton again and was surprised to see a faint sheen on the man's forehead, and his face seemed to have grown even redder. His clothes were always stylish and crisply laundered, but the shirt he was wearing now looked moist under the arms, and Jared suddenly wondered if the teacher was coming down with something. The flu, maybe?

Mr. Keaton cleared his throat, then continued more strongly. "There are some very real gaps in Jared's understanding of basic concepts and strategies that prevent him from . . ."

Jared let the words flow over and around him. They were talking like he wasn't even there. He could probably go shoot some hoops right now and they wouldn't even miss him. He thought about how, at noon, he and Steve had played one on one, forgetting for a few minutes what the afternoon would bring. He remembered one particular shot, how he'd faked right—which Steve had anticipated—and then followed his fake, leaping into the air, the ball leaving his fingertips, climbing clear of Steve's hands and swishing through—

"Jared?"

"Huh?"

"Earth to Jared." His mother shook her head. To the teacher she said, "Is this what he's like in class?"

Keaton grinned. Not like a teacher, though. Like a kid. Almost goofy. "No," he said, "not most of the time." Even the roots of his hair seemed to be turning red. "But he can get this way during math sometimes. Can't you, Jared?"

Now it was Jared's turn to flush. "Yes, sir," he mumbled.

"In case you didn't hear him, Mr. Keaton has a suggestion that might help," his mother said.

Jared was pretty sure they didn't mean a brain transplant and, aside from that, he didn't think there was much anyone could do. "What?" he sighed.

The teacher was still looking at his mother. Then, with what seemed like a tremendous effort, he turned toward Jared. "Cornwallis has an after-school tutorial program that pairs students who have difficulties in a particular area with students who have demonstrated strengths in that area. It takes the first five or six weeks of school to identify both groups of students, and we're just about ready to begin the program again. I'd like to pair you up with a student who is especially strong in math."

Jared gave his teacher a startled look. "Pair me up?"

"You'll work one on one with that student at least three afternoons a week. Or, if you wish, you can work fewer afternoons and spend some time together on weekends."

"Look, Mr. Keaton, I had a tutor last year. It didn't help much. Mom'll tell you that."

The teacher wasn't deterred. "I know. I saw it in your file. But that tutor was an adult, and adults who aren't in the classroom working daily with the material often don't have a clear sense of what problems exist. That's why this program has worked so well here. Students who are learning the concepts usually understand better than adults what things can trip up another student. And," he continued, "because teachers meet with the tutors on a regular basis, they can monitor how things are going and suggest ways to overcome any difficulties."

"Why can't I just get extra help from you?" Jared said, a pained expression on his face.

The teacher grinned. "Oh, you're *still* going to get extra help from me. Don't you worry about that. You know I spend every noon break in my classroom, working with students who ask for extra help."

Jared groaned inwardly. Yes, he knew that only too well. But it interfered with noon basketball on the courts behind the school.

His mother turned to him. "So, Jared," she said, placing

a hand on his, "what do you think? Are we going to give this a try?"

Jared sat quietly for a moment. He knew he didn't have a choice, but he at least wanted to maintain the illusion that he did. And who knew? Maybe it would work. As long as it didn't interfere with basketball, he guessed it was worth a shot. He almost grinned at his unintentional pun. "Okay," he said finally. "Who are you pairin' me up with?"

Jared could see a twinkle in Mr. Keaton's eyes as he spoke. "A wonderful student. She's in your class. Ellie Brejovic."

CHAPTER 5

"*Uh*-uh," Jared said, shaking his head fiercely. "No *way!*" He forced the words through clenched teeth as he stormed ahead of his mother across the school parking lot toward the bus stop.

"Jared—" his mother began, but he cut her off.

"Don't even *think* about it!" he spat. But his tirade was directed more at himself than at his mother. "Tutored by *her*? Right. I can just see it now . . ." If his classes that day had been a blur, that was nothing compared with the fog he sat through once Keaton dropped his bombshell. Jared hadn't heard another word of the conversation. Images of Ellie yawning over a math book while he struggled to solve some lousy problem about best buys or sales tax blocked everything else from his mind. Smelly Ellie: his *tutor!* Right.

His mom let him work off some steam before she spoke again. "It's not like you have a choice, you know."

Jared turned to her, a pleading note in his voice now. "I'll get extra help from Mr. Keaton every day from now on," he said. "I'll do extra homework. I'll . . . I'll . . ."

His mother shook her head. "I've heard all those promises before, and look where they've gotten you. Right here, my friend." She sighed. "Look, there's nothing to be embarrassed about. All kinds of people have trouble with math. Your father did."

Jared shot her a look that would have wilted flowers, then kept walking. A dead-beat dad who had run out on them when Jared was four wasn't an example that would make anyone feel like cheering. He scowled even more darkly.

His mother seemed to realize her mistake and tried another tack. "Mr. Keaton didn't say it was for all year. Just until you get a better handle on things."

Jared grunted. Nothing she could say was going to make him feel better.

"Okay," she said, "I didn't want to do this, but you've forced me into it. No tutor, no tryout."

Jared whirled to face her. "You can't *do* that!"

"Just watch me, buster. Remember when you wanted to join soccer? Cornwallis students need a parent to sign a permission form if they want to join a team. And the last time I checked, I was the only one still around."

Jared's mother kept walking, her head held high. Jared recognized that walk. Once his mother squared her shoulders and straightened her back like an iron rail, there was no swaying her.

For the very first time, a part of him hoped he *didn't* make Jamieson's team.

* * *

Steve couldn't have been more sympathetic. After he'd stopped laughing, that is. Two seconds after Jared shared Mr. Keaton's news about who'd be tutoring him, Steve was on his back on Jared's lawn, rocking back and forth, holding his stomach as he cackled and snorted. Even Cal was looking at Steve like he'd lost his mind.

"Thanks a lot." Jared scowled when Steve finally choked back his laughter and crawled to his feet.

"Sorry, Jared. Really." He wiped his face with the back of his sleeve, managed to make a couple more chuckles sound like hiccups, and then shook his head. "Out of all the people who are in that tutor program, why'd Keaton have to match you up with *her*?"

Steve was right. In a school of over five hundred sixth-, seventh-, and eighth-graders, surely there had to be at least one other tutor Jared could have worked with.

"That's what *I* wanted to know," Jared grumbled. Since he hadn't heard much else that Mr. Keaton had said during the meeting, he'd asked his mother that same question on the bus ride home. "Keaton *says* it's because she's the absolute best math student he's ever had," Jared told Steve. He shook his head, self-pity settling firmly on both his shoulders. "Which, I guess, means I'm the absolute *worst* math student he's ever had." He kicked dispiritedly at the grass, which had yellowed during one of the driest falls on record. Apparently, he thought, there were records for everything. Including bad luck. And the winner is . . .

"But you're still tryin' out for the Cougars, right?" When Jared didn't answer, Steve moved around to face him. "Look, this is a rotten break, but you ain't gonna throw away the tryouts, are you?" He waited another moment. "'Cause that'd be the *dumbest* thing ever, right?"

Jared stared at the ground. Hadn't he already *proven* to everyone just how dumb he was? Now the idea of getting tutored by Ellie Brejovic cranked "dumb" up a couple of notches to a whole new level. He could just imagine the looks on people's faces when *that* piece of information got around, could see Rafe Wells and his buddies sniggering about it, making stupid remarks loud enough for Jared to hear.

Like Jared had done last Saturday in the deli.

"Yeah," Jared replied, almost to himself, "that'd be pretty dumb all right."

Steve clapped his friend on the shoulder. "Cheer up. It could be worse."

"How?"

Steve's smile faltered. He had no answer for that question.

CHAPTER 6

"Look," Jared muttered the following afternoon, "I figure we gotta do this just till the basketball tryouts are over. But as soon as Jamieson posts the roster and I ain't on it, we're quits. You got that?"

Ellie Brejovic shrugged. "Look, I'm only doing this for my extracurricular credit."

So *that's* how you're gonna get it, Jared thought. At *my* expense. Just great.

"So the sooner we're through," Ellie continued, "the better."

Jared raised his eyebrows. Those were the most words Ellie had ever spoken to him at one time, even counting last year, when they were in grade five together and had been assigned to the same group to research volcanoes. Except everyone in the group just sat back and let Ellie do all the work. Along with typing a five-page report (complete with footnotes), designing a detailed poster illustrating the life cycle of a typical volcano, and recording an audiotape with sounds of volcanic activity she'd downloaded off the Internet, Ellie built a scale model of Mount St. Helens, showing what the mountain looked like before and after its surprise eruption in 1980. All by herself. Jared and the other three group members chatted and fooled around and pretty much just enjoyed themselves. And accepted the A+ their teacher gave to all of them.

"Yeah, well, just so you know, okay?" He'd agonized the whole day about their after-school meeting, dreading that Ellie might turn around in her seat in class and make some comment to him about it. Fortunately, she hadn't, and he wanted to make sure she knew the ground rules for these sessions. *His* ground rules.

He stepped back and opened the kitchen door wider to let her in. He poked his head out just long enough to see whether anyone had noticed her, then ducked back inside. Not, however, before he saw Steve flash him a thumbs-up from his kitchen window. Jared saw the tip of Cal's tail wagging beside Steve. After promising he'd never breathe a word about Ellie coming to Jared's house,

Steve had offered to keep the dog out of their hair during the tutorial session. Unlike normal dogs, who growled at people they didn't know, Cal tended to slobber over strangers.

"Where do we do this?" Ellie asked. Straight to the point. She was still holding her bookbag (loaded, Jared suspected, with tutor torture-tools), waiting for him to tell her where she could put it.

He ignored the temptation to say what sprang to his mind. "There," he said, pointing at the kitchen table.

Ellie took off her jacket, pulled out a chair, and sat down.

Jared's mother was in the spare bedroom. Although it was little more than a closet with a window, she used the room as an office, where she kept important papers and files. She'd been in there nearly half an hour balancing her bankbook and writing cheques to pay at least some of their bills, and Jared now heard her close the drawer of the small filing cabinet. A moment later, she appeared in the doorway. "Hello, Ellie. I'm Jared's mom."

"Hi," Ellie said. Nothing else. It was as if, knowing the arrangement was temporary, she didn't need to bother being friendly. Or didn't know how.

But Jared knew her abruptness wouldn't faze his mother, who had told him half a dozen times how grateful she was—as he should be—that Mr. Keaton had set up the tutoring. And the fact that it was free was a welcome bonus for her bank account. "I want to thank you for doing this," his mother said. "Jared can really use the help."

"Right," Ellie said. A silence followed, during which Jared sadly contemplated Ellie's large bookbag.

"Mr. Keaton speaks very highly of you," his mother continued, and Jared groaned inwardly. He knew his mother all right, had heard from her co-workers, who stopped by now and then, how she could thaw even the most aloof patients. She wouldn't give up until she'd made some sort of connection with Ellie.

This time it worked. Ellie softened. "He's a great teacher," she said shyly.

Apparently satisfied at last, Jared's mother said, "Well, I'll leave the two of you alone. If you get hungry, there's fruit on the counter, and juice is in the fridge." She returned to her tiny office.

Jared expected Ellie to make some comment about the fridge, an ancient flea-market purchase that shuddered each time the compressor kicked in and wheezed constantly until it shut off, but Ellie said nothing. Instead, she reached into her bookbag and pulled out the math binder Mr. Keaton had everyone keep. Unlike Jared's, Ellie's binder was up-to-date and organized. And neat. She opened it to page one.

Jared glanced at the clock on the wall and sighed.

* * *

"Hour's up," Jared said, nodding toward the clock. He'd been watching the minute hand crawl toward five o'clock while Ellie played with bingo chips.

Jared had never seen bingo chips before, only those daubers that people marked their game cards with, but somewhere Ellie had found a package of small plastic discs that apparently were used in pre-dauber times. Some were red and some were blue, and Ellie had been using them to show Jared how to add positive and negative numbers, which Mr. Keaton had done a lesson on that day.

Jared had understood since fourth grade how people needed something besides positive numbers to show things like below-zero temperatures and overdrawn bank accounts—he'd certainly seen his mother's negative bank balance enough times to know the significance of that. But he'd gotten confused when he tried to combine both positive and negative figures. Mr. Keaton had shown the class how to use a number line to do this, but several times Jared got lost making his pencil jump back and forth on the line he had drawn in his binder. After he'd done almost the entire page of homework wrong, Ellie had pulled bingo chips out of her bookbag and told Jared to think of the blue ones as negative numbers and the red ones as positive. Then she'd shown him how one blue and one red combined to make zero. He'd felt like an idiot moving the plastic chips around on the table, and he was so bored he'd tried to use mind control to move the clock's minute hand ahead faster. It didn't work, and their first sixty-minute session had seemed like six hours. Finally, though, it was over.

As if on cue, Jared's mother reappeared. "Would you like to stay for supper, Ellie?" she asked. "The least I can do is make you a meal for all your help."

Jared frowned at the prospect of spending even more time with Ellie, and once again tried mind control, this time to make the girl voice the words he wanted to hear.

"No, thanks," she said.

Yes! thought Jared. *It worked!*

Ellie gathered up her materials and began packing her bag. She seemed to want to leave as much as Jared wanted her out the door. A couple of the bingo chips fell to the floor, and Jared reached down to get them. Ellie stooped to get the chips at exactly the same moment, and their heads bonked together with a sound like coconuts colliding. For a moment Jared saw stars, and he was surprised when Ellie didn't even say "ow." Thick skull, he thought.

Thankfully, minutes later she was gone.

His mother reached into the fridge and took out a package of boneless chicken breasts while Jared cleared away his math homework and set the table. "So, how'd it go?" she asked as she began slicing the chicken into strips. The question seemed casual, but Jared could tell she was dying for details.

He sniffed. "Okay."

"Just okay?"

"Mom!"

"All right, all right," she said. "This is me minding my own business." She finished slicing the chicken and placed the pieces in a baking pan, then slid the pan into the oven. "I'm just glad you're taking this tutoring seriously." He could hear her humming as she got carrots and potatoes out of the crisper.

Taking this tutoring seriously. Yeah, right. Like it would do any good anyway. He spied another bingo chip on the floor and scowled. Reaching down, he scooped it up, looked at it for a moment, then tossed it toward the wastebasket on the other side of the kitchen. It landed squarely in the centre and, for the thousandth time, he wished he could do math as easily as he could sink a shot. Then he wouldn't have to put up with Smelly Ellie Brejovic and these after-school sessions. She'd have to find some *other* math victim to earn her extracurricular credit with.

He smiled grimly. At least Coach Jamieson's tryouts began in two days. Once they were over, he'd put an end to this tutoring crap for good.

CHAPTER 7

"So, how'd things go with Ellie?" Steve asked under his breath on the bus to school the next morning. "Learn anything?"

"That they didn't always use bingo daubers," Jared replied.

"Huh?"

Jared shrugged. "Nothin'. It was a waste of time. Just like I knew it would be."

Steve shook his head. "Sorry, buddy."

"Don't be. At least I won't have to do it for long."

They rode in silence for a while before Steve spoke again. "So, what was it like workin' with her? She hard to talk to?"

"As long as she was talkin' math, she was fine. Believe

me, we didn't talk about anything else. She's a walkin' textbook, man."

"But she didn't help you any?" Steve asked.

Jared sighed and turned toward the window. "When it comes to math, even a walkin' textbook can't help *me*."

The bus pulled to a stop in front of the school. Before heading off in different directions toward their homerooms, Steve and Jared made plans to meet, as usual, on the outdoor basketball courts at lunchtime.

The main entrance of Cornwallis Middle School, the one closest to Keaton's classroom, reminded Jared of a lighthouse. The architect had created a three-storey atrium with windows from floor to ceiling that captured both morning and afternoon sunlight. On fine days, light flooded the entrance and the corridors that stretched beyond it. Last winter, Jared's mom had bought a million-candlepower rechargeable flashlight that, she once joked, could sear the retinas of an eagle. Stepping inside the atrium on a bright day was like suddenly being trapped inside that beam. It always took a few seconds for Jared's dazzled eyes to adjust.

"Hey, Jared."

He turned to see Samantha Solomon and Erica Longmire standing next to their lockers. They were in 6C, the class across the hall from his, and although Jared didn't know them well, they always made a point of saying hi. They giggled and blushed a lot and usually talked about things he wasn't much interested in—clothes, hair colour—but at least they could talk about something besides math.

"Hey," Jared returned.

"I heard you're gonna try out for the Cougars tomorrow," said Erica.

Jared nodded. "Don't imagine I'll make the cut but, yeah, I'm gonna try."

Samantha lightly brushed his arm with her fingertips. "Oh, I think you've got a *great* chance, Jared. You're a natural. We've watched you on the courts at lunchtime."

It was Jared's turn to blush. "Um . . . thanks." He hadn't realized he'd had an audience.

"And you've been playin' some great soccer, too," Samantha continued. "I've been to all your games." She touched his arm again, this time letting her hand linger a moment before pulling it away.

Jared felt his ears turn pink. He might be a natural on the soccer field and basketball court, but he was a novice when it came to talking to girls. He groped for something to say.

"Geek alert," Erica said.

For a moment, Jared thought she was talking about him, and he flushed again. But then he turned in the direction she was looking and saw Ellie coming down the hallway, her bookbag seemingly twice as heavy as everyone else's. He stifled a groan.

"Pu-leeze," said Samantha behind her raised hand, "how many books does a person *need* at one time?"

Erica snickered, the sound thin and brittle in the near-empty hallway.

They watched as Ellie came toward them, her eyes focused on some spot just in front of her face. She didn't even glance at the three as she passed by and turned into Mr. Keaton's classroom. But there was no way she could have missed hearing Erica's next remark. "That one takes *nerd* to a whole new level."

Jared snorted along with Samantha at the comment, anxious to show the girls that, while Ellie Brejovic and he might be classmates, they certainly weren't friends. He'd worried all night about what this morning might bring. He'd worried that people might somehow find out about the tutoring. He'd worried that Mr. Keaton might ask him in front of the others how things had gone, even though the tutoring was supposed to be confidential. He'd even worried that Ellie might expect him to talk to her about it at school. He hadn't slept much.

Well, at least now he didn't think he had to worry about Ellie talking to him about it.

Jared stayed chatting with the two girls until the warning bell rang, pretending to be interested in the fake fingernails Erica had just gotten at Top-to-Toe, a new beauty boutique at the mall. Jared actually thought the nails looked a little creepy—he couldn't imagine Erica being able to brush her teeth with them on, let alone play her flute in band or take part in gym class—but even listening to her ramble on about fake fingernails was better than going to his classroom any sooner than absolutely necessary.

He slipped in the door just as the final bell rang. Sitting at his computer, Mr. Keaton glanced at his watch and frowned. "I almost recorded you as absent, Jared. Two more seconds and I'd have e-mailed your name to the office."

"Sorry," Jared said as he moved quickly toward his seat.

Ellie, sitting at the desk in front of his, didn't look up as he passed.

* * *

"Negative five?" Jared offered tentatively. He hated being put on the spot during math period, and he'd kept his face down and pretended to be calculating when Mr. Keaton asked for volunteers to evaluate the integer question on the board. But Keaton didn't always wait for students to volunteer, and Jared was the first person he'd called on.

"Are you sure about that?" asked the teacher.

Jared, of course, wasn't sure about anything, but over the years he'd found it was usually easier to say he was. That way, it was up to the teacher to prove him wrong. "Yes, I'm sure," he said.

Mr. Keaton smiled. "Good, because you're right."

A murmur from the back of the room revealed that others were as surprised as Jared that he was correct. Jared heard Rafe Wells's voice in that murmur.

"Can you tell us how you got that?" Mr. Keaton asked.

Jared swallowed. He'd found it hard to concentrate all day, thinking instead of the first basketball tryout to be held the next afternoon. But he'd forced himself to watch the teacher work out a few examples on the board, and he'd started thinking about those bingo chips again, remembering what Ellie had said about them. She'd called the blue chips negative since below-zero temperatures turned your skin blue, and the red chips were positive because stove elements turned red when they got hot. When you put one red and one blue together, she'd said, they combined to make a zero, so when you added a whole bunch of reds and blues together, you just had to ask yourself two questions: which did you have more of—red or blue—and how many more did you have than the other? It sort of made sense, in a weird kind of way.

"Well, Jared?" Mr. Keaton prompted again. "Care to share with us how you got negative five?"

Jared felt his face heat up, and he looked at the board again. Suddenly, all the numbers—both positive and negative—looked the same, and he found himself wondering what he could have seen in the problem in the first place. *Bingo chips?* Sure. Like bingo chips could be the answer to all his math problems. How dumb could he be?

"Jared?"

"Lucky guess," Jared mumbled.

He looked down at his paper and longed for tomorrow afternoon.

CHAPTER 8

"Nervous?" Steve whispered as they changed into their gym gear. Now that Jamieson's tryouts were finally here, Steve seemed much more subdued than usual.

He wasn't the only one. The locker room was filled with boys getting ready, but you wouldn't know it from listening at the door. Usually, the room echoed with noise, guys kidding each other, joking around, snapping each other with shorts or towels, bragging about nonsense, but today most of the sounds came from gym bags being zipped open or closed, sneakers hitting the floor, locker doors clanging shut. Everyone was subdued, lost in thought, even the eighth-graders who'd made the team last year in grade seven. With Coach Jamieson, there were no guarantees.

Jared nodded.

"Me, too," his friend said.

"Yeah, well, at least you know what to expect. You tried out before."

"And didn't make the cut," Steve reminded him.

Jared sat on the bench and began tying his sneakers. They were almost too tight, but there was still some wear left in them. At least, that's what his mother had told him when he'd asked on Monday about getting a new pair. "Try not to grow for the next few weeks," she'd joked with him. His last trip to Value Village for clothes had pretty much exhausted their limited resources. And this morning had brought yet another unexpected expense. He and his mom had gotten out of bed to discover that their old Kenmore had broken down during the night. Not wanting to chance eating the now almost room-temperature food, they'd had to throw a lot of it out, and the rest they'd carried over to Steve's house.

Jared felt Steve tap him on the shoulder. When he looked up, he saw his friend nod toward the doorway. Jared turned to see Rafe saunter in wearing a warm-up suit and sneakers that looked like they cost nearly as much as the refrigerator in the Sears flyer his mom had ordered before she left for work.

"Gentlemen," Rafe said to the room in general. He sounded like he was thirty years old and running for prime minister.

Jared and Steve nodded at him, as did several of the others in the locker room. Even the eighth-graders.

Steve rarely said anything negative about other people, but he sometimes broke that rule when it came to Rafe. He leaned over to Jared and muttered, "Takes after his old man. I seen him on the news a couple times. The guy's all about image."

Rafe came over and stood by Jared. "Looks like you and I and Kyle and Pete are the only grade sixes trying out," he said. Jared noticed how he'd said "you and I" and not "you and me." The thirty-year-old thing again.

"Looks that way," Jared said.

Rafe smiled, his teeth as straight and even as piano keys. As white, too. But his eyes weren't smiling. "Good luck," he said.

"You too," Jared returned, watching Rafe move off. He seemed to glide rather than walk across the floor. Jared half expected him to reach out and shake a few hands before heading out to the gymnasium.

Steve clapped a hand on Jared's shoulder. "He's just tryin' to psych you out, buddy."

"And doin' a great job," Jared muttered.

Steve poked him in the ribs. "Look, you're just as good a player as he is. I've got the bruises to prove it."

Jared grinned. He could always count on Steve for a boost.

"C'mon, buddy," Steve said as he stood up. "Let's you and me kick some major basketball butt."

* * *

The tryout seemed to last forever. Coach Jamieson put them through their paces, and it was soon obvious who was really serious about the game and who just wanted the glory of making the team. After the forty-two boys had warmed up, Jamieson began barking out drill after drill, from the go behind and the backdoor cut to the catch and shoot and the full-court three on two. Everyone had to hustle to keep up. By the end of the first hour, one of the less experienced players had simply walked off the court, and two more followed a half hour later. Jamieson thanked them for showing up, but everyone knew that he was really thanking them for not wasting his time.

Following the drills, Jamieson had them scrimmage, and it didn't take long for Rafe to prove that the expensive basketball camps he'd attended that past summer were worth every cent his father had paid for them. Jamieson put him and Jared on opposing teams, and Rafe deftly stole the ball from him four different times, forcing Jared to shift quickly from offensive to defensive manoeuvres. It was only Jared's longer legs and greater speed that enabled him to make stops on two of his four turnarounds. The other two times, Rafe wove neatly through the defence and scored impressive baskets. Even a couple of the grade eight students shook their heads in admiration. More than once when Jared was subbed off, he saw Jamieson write something on his clipboard after watching Rafe execute a particular play.

It was tough, but the longer they went and the harder it got to put one foot in front of the other, the more Jared loved it. Sweat burned his eyes, his legs ached from the constant running and twisting and jumping, and his breathing was often little more than a laboured wheeze, but he liked the challenge, enjoyed forcing himself, was surprised and pleased to see just what his body could do. From time to time his eyes sought out Steve, and he could tell his friend was loving every minute, too. They'd grin and flash each other a thumbs-up and then keep going.

At the end of two and a half hours, Jamieson called all the boys to the centre of the gymnasium, where he had them sit in a circle on the floor. His face was difficult to read. He almost never smiled, and his eyes looked as if they could burn through concrete. But they could tell he was pleased with what he'd seen. "You guys worked hard for me this afternoon," he said. "And you get to do it all again tomorrow."

The boys groaned, but they'd known what to expect.

He looked around the circle. "There's a lot of talent

here. A *lot* of talent." He paused, allowing them a moment to appreciate the praise. Pete nudged Rafe and Rafe smiled broadly. As much as Jared didn't care for him, he thought Rafe had every right to be pleased with himself. He'd been phenomenal out on the court.

"And now that I've seen what skills you have," the coach continued, "I need to see how you work together as a team. One person doesn't win a basketball game." He let that final comment hang in the air for a moment, then pointed to the locker room. "Take a long shower. You deserve it."

* * *

"Oh, man, I don't think I'll be able to *move* in the morning," Steve said as he climbed onto the bus. Both he and Jared were already stiff and sore, and they moved like astronauts in lunar gravity, slow and deliberate.

Jared moaned in agreement as they settled into a seat. "And this was just a *tryout*," he said. "What are the actual *practices* like?"

"I heard last year that Cougars lose five pounds the first week of the season," said Steve. "Jamieson puts 'em though the wringer—running, strength training, aerobics, the works."

Jared grinned at him. "Lemme get this straight. We *want* this, right?"

"More than life itself," Steve sighed, closing his eyes.

Jared yawned loudly. "I think I'm gonna crash as soon as I finish supper," he said.

Steve opened one eye. "Aren't you forgettin' something?"

"What?"

"Isn't tonight tutor-time?"

Jared moaned again. "Shoot. Me. Now."

CHAPTER 9

Cal was keeping Ellie company on the back step when Jared got home. His mother was still at work, so no one had been home to greet Ellie when she arrived at six o'clock. Jared glanced at his watch—quarter past. Jeez! What if somebody'd *seen* her? Steve was the only person from school who lived in his neighbourhood, but anybody could have been passing by. Jared's eyes darted up and down the block to see if anyone was watching, but there was only Steve hauling himself stiffly up his back steps. Steve nodded at him, then went inside.

"Sorry I'm late," Jared muttered as he fumbled for the key in his pocket. Standing there by the door, he suddenly remembered standing in the school hallway with Samantha and Erica the morning before, remembered the way he had laughed at Erica's comment about nerds. Awkwardness washed over him, and he felt like he should say more. "Tryouts took longer than I—"

"Let's just get started, okay?" said Ellie. "I have a lot to do tonight."

Sure you do, thought Jared with a flash of irritation. Important stuff, too, I bet. Like alphabetizing today's vocabulary words or colour-coding your math quizzes. He unlocked the door, then turned to untie Cal. They followed the dog inside. Or tried to. Cal couldn't seem to get close enough to Ellie, licking her hand and dancing by her side. Just once, Jared thought, I wish you'd act like a normal dog. Maybe even growl once or twice.

As if in response, Jared's stomach growled noisily, and he realized how long it had been since lunchtime. Leaving his gym bag and backpack on the bench just inside the door, he crossed the kitchen and opened the fridge door, then scowled.

"What's the matter?" Ellie asked.

"I forgot. Our fridge broke last night." He stared at the empty shelves as if doing so would somehow make food appear out of thin air. A hollow knot was forming in the pit of his stomach. He closed the door, then noticed a piece of paper on the kitchen table, along with a ten-dollar bill. It was a note from his mother: *Here's money to buy yourself supper. Something healthy, okay?* She had underlined "healthy" twice. *See you when I get home. I want to hear all about your tryout. Love, Mom.* As always, she'd drawn a happy face at the bottom with a big J for a nose. "Jared faces," she used to call those drawings when he was barely old enough to hold a pencil himself. There was a PS beside the Jared face: *Don't forget Ellie is coming today.* It seemed everyone had remembered but him.

His stomach rumbled again, even louder than before, and he felt his face flush with embarrassment. He noisily got Cal's food out of the cupboard, hoping the crinkling of the dog food bag would mask the rumbling of his stomach. He poured some of the dry nuggets into Cal's dish, then got the dog some fresh water. When he'd finished, he turned. "All set?" he asked. He was answered by a loud gurgle in his belly.

Ellie said nothing, but he thought he saw the edges of her mouth twitch as she took off her jacket and hung it over the back of a chair, then sat down at the kitchen table. She busied herself opening her bookbag while another sound from the symphony in his stomach—this one a long warble—resonated through the kitchen. Jared quickly grabbed a chair and pulled it away from the table, but the scraping of its legs across the worn tile did little to camouflage the noise. Red-faced, he made a production of coughing and clearing his throat as sat down and reached for the paper and pencils his mother had left on the table, but then his stomach released a high-pitched whine that made Cal look up from his dish and cock his head, searching for the source of the sound. *Jeez!*

"You have some canned soup around?" Ellie asked softly as she continued to root around in her bag. "Wouldn't take long to heat it up."

Jared shook his head. "My mom left me some money for supper. I'll grab some pizza at Luigi's after we finish." His stomach growled again. It sounded like Cal begging for dog biscuits.

Her eyes still focused on her bag, Ellie asked, "What about Kraft Dinner? You have any of that?"

Who'd she think she was? His *babysitter*? "Look, you wanna get at this math or what?"

She looked at him and shrugged. "Up to you."

* * *

Fifteen minutes later, it sounded like a cruise missile was roaring through Jared's stomach. His ears were on fire, and he could barely concentrate on the stuff Ellie was telling him about perimeter, area, and volume.

She looked up from the math papers spread out on the kitchen table and sighed. "Look," she said, "maybe you should get something to eat now."

"You mean forget about tutoring for tonight?" he asked, suddenly hopeful.

She frowned. "No. Mr. Keaton says tutors have to volunteer at least three hours each week. We're not even halfway through today's session yet."

Jared glanced at the clock on the wall and ground his teeth to hide his disappointment. But as hungry as he was, no *way* was he going to be seen out in public with *her*. "Let's just do this," he said, forcing himself to look at the math again. His stomach burbled.

Ellie pushed her chair back from the table. "You never said about the Kraft Dinner. Do you have any?"

Jared shrugged. "I dunno. I guess so." He got up, opened a cupboard door, and pulled out a package of the macaroni and cheese mix. His mother made it only when she was in a rush. Right now, however, it seemed like a banquet in a box.

Ellie stood up and took the box from him. "Where are your pots?" she asked.

He raised his eyebrows. "You're gonna cook?"

She sighed. "Just get me a pot."

He got her one and she filled it with water and placed it on the stove, turning on the burner. "Ever hear of killing two birds with one stone?" she asked.

"Who hasn't?" he said, glumly.

She shook the box of Kraft Dinner and the dry noodles rattled inside. "This," she said, "is the stone." She returned to the table, peeled back the top of the box, and poured some of the noodles into her hand. Standing the box on its end, she made a ring of noodles around the outside of the package. "See how the noodles go all the way around the box?" she asked.

"I ain't blind," Jared muttered.

"Lay them out in a straight line," she told him.

He was annoyed. "Are we cookin' or doin' math?"

She sighed. "Both. Just do it."

He laid the noodles end to end.

"How long is the row?" she asked.

He looked at her as if she were losing her mind, then reached for a ruler and measured. "Twenty-six centimetres," he said.

"That's the perimeter of one end of the box," Ellie told him.

Jared stared at her. "That's perimeter?"

She nodded, then poured the noodles back into the box and passed it to him. "Is the box full?" she asked.

"You know it ain't," he said. He didn't try to hide the irritation in his voice.

"Got a measuring cup?" Ellie asked.

He was about to ask her who the heck *didn't* have one, but he clenched his teeth instead and got a measuring cup from a shelf above the stove and set it on the table. She poured the noodles into it. "How much of the noodles do you have?"

He frowned. "About 200 millilitres. Why?"

"How many of that amount would you need to fill the box to the top?"

He scratched his head and looked inside the box again. "I dunno. Two times that. Maybe three."

"How much would that be altogether?"

He was reaching for his calculator when she stopped him. "You don't need that," she said. "Do it in your head."

He was about to tell her he'd darned well use his calculator if he wanted to, then realized he really didn't need it for those numbers. He told her the total.

"That's the volume of the box," Ellie said.

By now, the water was boiling on the stove. She stood up and dumped the noodles into the pan, then pressed some buttons on her digital watch. She sat down again, pulled out the package of dried cheese, and pushed the empty box toward Jared. "Take the box apart and lay all the different pieces flat."

Jared's stomach gurgled. "How long are we gonna play with this stuff?" he sighed.

"Till we've finished," Ellie told him.

Jared scowled but began ripping the box apart and laying the pieces of cardboard on the table.

"How many square centimetres of packaging would you say you have there?" she asked.

He frowned. "There's so many pieces," he said.

"You can move them around if you want. Try fitting them together like a puzzle."

He began sliding the pieces of the package around on

the table until they again formed a crude rectangle. When he'd finished, he estimated how many square centimetres were in the rectangle.

"That," Ellie explained, "is the area of the box." Her watch beeped. "And that," she said, "is supper."

* * *

Even without milk to mix with it, Kraft Dinner had never tasted so good. Jared drained the noodles and mixed in the butter and cheese powder in record time. He'd offered some to Ellie but she'd said, "No thanks," so he'd practically inhaled the whole pot himself.

While he ate, Ellie asked him to tell her about what he'd done with the noodles and the package. After that, she asked him what he knew about measurement now that he didn't know before.

To tell the truth, there wasn't a lot he'd known before. He'd mixed up perimeter, area, and volume more times than he could remember, but now he thought he had a better handle on them. But he still couldn't figure out how to calculate the volume of things you couldn't measure with a cup—like a really big box or even a room like the kitchen—and she reminded him how to measure length, width, and height and then multiply them to get cubic units. She reached into her bag and pulled out a handful of Lego pieces that were shaped like cubes. He recalled Mr. Keaton talking about cubic units the week before, but he hadn't really understood what the teacher meant. Now he thought maybe he did.

Ellie spent the rest of the hour reviewing with Jared the things they'd talked about during their first session. Then she gave him a sheet of integer questions to try. He made only one mistake.

"Gee, Jared, you did great!" she told him. "You didn't get *any* right on Tuesday."

Embarrassed, he mumbled, "I remembered the bingo chips. That helped."

Ellie glanced at the clock on the wall and was clearly surprised at the time. "I have to go." She stooped and patted Cal, who had been lying at her feet since he'd finished his meal, then stood up and slipped on her jacket.

Jared got up, too. He felt awkward, unsure what to say. "Thanks for the help."

"No problem." She opened the door.

"I'll see—" Jared began, then stopped.

She turned. "What?"

He shrugged, embarrassed by what he'd almost said. "Nothin'."

She looked at him for a moment, then nodded and closed the door behind her.

Jared watched her through the window as she walked down the driveway, her heavy bookbag over her shoulder making her look like one of those Sherpas he'd seen on a

Discovery Channel program about Mount Everest. The Sherpas, from the mountainous country of Nepal, lived at a higher elevation than anyone else in the world. Their strength and mountaineering skills made them invaluable to climbers, who'd been hiring them as guides and assistants since the mid-1900s. Watching the television program, Jared had been awed by the remoteness of their life, and had wondered if the Sherpas ever felt lonely in that harsh mountain region.

For the first time, he found himself wondering if Ellie ever felt lonely. There were things other than mountains that could set people apart. Walls had a way of being built without anyone ever seeing them. Like the wall around Ellie in their classroom.

He thought about her standing in the doorway a moment ago. Out of habit, he'd started to say "I'll see you tomorrow." But, of course, that wasn't entirely true. She'd sit at her desk, working or reading, while he and every other kid in 6K would pretend she wasn't even there.

CHAPTER 10

Standing outside the door of Mr. Keaton's classroom, Jared saw Rafe sitting at his desk, talking to Kyle and Pete. From the hallway, Jared couldn't make out what Rafe was saying, but he could tell the three were talking about the basketball tryout the day before. Or rather, Rafe was talking and the other two were listening intently, their eyes glued to Rafe's hands as they made ball-handling motions in the air.

No wonder Kyle and Pete were mesmerized, Jared thought. After yesterday's scrimmage, he knew Rafe had an excellent chance of making the team. If Coach Jamieson *did* pick a sixth-grader, Rafe would probably be the one.

"Good morning, Jared."

Jared turned to see Mr. Keaton holding the black leather briefcase he carried to class each day. Most of the students in 6K referred to it as "the black hole" because there seemed to be no end to the work the teacher could pull out of it. Many of them complained vigorously about the number of assignments the teacher gave them, but most of them liked Mr. Keaton. He made his lessons interesting, and he treated everyone in the same fair manner. Even as annoyed as Jared was at him for arranging the tutoring, Jared had to admit he was one of the best teachers he'd ever had.

"Morning, Mr. Keaton."

"How was the tryout?"

That was another thing Jared liked about the teacher: the way he took a real interest in his students' activities, whether school related or not. "Brutal," said Jared.

The teacher smiled. "So Mr. Jamieson hasn't mellowed since last year, eh?"

Jared grinned in return. "No," he said. "He really worked us."

Still smiling, Mr. Keaton patted his briefcase. "I'm going to do the same today," he said. "Surprise quiz."

Jared's face fell. "Math?" he groaned.

The teacher nodded, then said quietly, "I'm interested to see if the tutoring has helped. How's it been going, anyway?"

Jared glanced around, but no one was within earshot.

He shrugged and studied his feet. "Who knows?" he mumbled. What else could he say? He hadn't had much trouble with the math homework the teacher had given them the day before, but that didn't mean anything. There'd been plenty of times when Jared thought he'd understood what they were doing in class, only to get back a quiz or an assignment and find out he'd done most of it wrong. Sometimes all of it.

"Give it time," Mr. Keaton said, patting Jared's shoulder as he moved past him into the classroom. "Rome wasn't built in a day."

Jared bit the inside of his cheek to keep from blurting, "Ya *think?*" A person would have to be an idiot to think that Rome—or *any* city, for that matter—could be built in a day. *Give it time.* There certainly wasn't a whole lot of that left, what with the final basketball tryouts being held that afternoon. If by some miracle he actually *did* make the team, his math mark would certainly keep him from playing anyway.

He stepped through the doorway and trudged toward his desk. As he passed Ellie's seat, he noticed she had her face buried in a book. She glanced up as he moved by her, but he ignored her and slumped heavily into his chair.

* * *

The final bell rang just as Jared passed his paper up to the front of his row. The morning and afternoon had dragged as he worried about the quiz, which Mr. Keaton had saved until the end of the day. There had been only one question, but it was a word problem—Jared hated those most of all—and it had taken him the full twenty minutes the teacher had given them to do it. The problem involved a man who wanted to plant an L-shaped flower garden and needed to know how many flowers he should buy to make a border and how much landscape fabric he needed to keep weeds from growing in the centre. Jared had no idea how to solve it, and at first he'd just turned his paper over and put his pencil down. Flowers and fabric. Jeez! Like any of it mattered.

But when he looked up, he saw Ellie glancing back, frowning at him. He considered giving her the finger, but he couldn't be bothered and just looked away. Watching the students around him looking at their papers, though, he remembered Mr. Keaton telling the class it was important to read a problem more than once. Reluctantly, he turned his paper back over and read the problem two more times, underlining words he thought might be important. Once he'd done that, he tried drawing the problem using the information he had underlined, and when he'd finished the picture, he found himself thinking about the things Ellie had done with the Kraft Dinner box and noodles. He wondered if he could do the same with the flowers and the landscape fabric and began jotting down numbers and thinking about whether he should add or multiply. He had just arrived at an answer when Mr. Keaton called for the quizzes.

"What'd you get for the part about the border?" he heard Kyle ask Rafe as they left the classroom. Jared strained to hear Rafe's reply, but it was lost in the sound of lockers opening and closing and feet heading toward exits and the outdoors beyond.

Jared sighed. It didn't matter. He'd probably got it wrong anyway, like all those other times.

"Why the long face, buddy?"

Jared turned to see Steve fall into step beside him, his gym bag slung over his shoulder. "Math quiz," Jared muttered.

Steve punched Jared's arm sympathetically. "Well, no use worryin' about it now. Plenty 'a time for that when you get it back, right?"

Jared nodded. Leave it to Steve to put things into perspective. Right now, he had something a whole lot better to think about. The final tryout. Even though he probably wouldn't make the team, he was going to play the next two and a half hours as if he already had. For that afternoon, at least, he would be a Cornwallis Cougar.

CHAPTER 11

"*You* check, okay?" Jared asked. He'd thought all weekend about the list going up that morning, but now he leaned against the wall on the other side of the hallway, refusing even to look at the paper tacked to the bulletin board beside the gymnasium doors. The paper around which thirty-seven other boys now jostled for position, craning their necks to see if their names were among the twelve on the list.

Steve nodded and flashed a thumbs-up for luck, but his usual grin was missing. In its place was an expression worn by people just before they dove into dark water.

Jared watched as his friend crossed the hall and threaded himself into the throng of bodies. Already some of the boys were pulling back, a few of them beaming with obvious pleasure but many of them shaking their heads or shrugging their shoulders. He saw Kyle and Pete shrugging and wasn't all that surprised they hadn't made the cut. Kyle and Pete were both excellent soccer players and outstanding forwards on their peewee hockey team, but strength alone wasn't enough on the basketball court. With more ball-handling practice, they'd probably make Jamieson's team next year.

But Jared *was* surprised to see Rafe roughly push his way out of the milling group, cursing under his breath. "I should've *made* that cut!" he snapped.

Kyle and Pete nodded vigorously. "You were one 'a the best out there, Rafe," Pete agreed. "Anyone could see that."

"Anyone with eyes and half a brain," Rafe seethed. "Jamieson's an *idiot!*"

Jared was conscious of a growing silence in the hallway. Coach Jamieson was standing in the doorway to the gymnasium but, with their backs turned, neither Rafe nor his two friends were aware of the teacher's presence. Someone noisily cleared his throat, but Rafe seemed oblivious to the warning.

"Scratch that," Rafe continued. "Jamieson would need monkey-brain injections just to *raise* his IQ to idiot."

Kyle snickered and Pete was in mid-guffaw when he stopped, suddenly acutely aware of the person behind them. "Hi, Mr. Jamieson," he gulped.

Rafe turned to face the teacher, and Jared was amazed at how coolly his classmate responded to the moment's awkwardness. "Hi, Mr. Jamieson," Rafe said, as if he'd been expecting the man to appear.

Coach Jamieson was blunt. "You have a problem with the list, Wells?"

Rafe flushed, but only for a moment. "Yes, I do," he said. "My name should be on it."

"You're right," the coach said. "Your name *should* be on it."

The man's statement clearly caught Rafe off guard, and Jared watched as satisfaction and surprise alternately flickered across the boy's face. "It should?" Rafe finally asked.

"Yes, it should," Jamieson replied. "And if I were looking only for ability in a player, it *would* be. You're good, Rafe. In fact, you've got some of the best technical skills I've ever seen in a player your age."

Rafe beamed, as Pete and Kyle clapped him on the shoulder. "That's what *we* was just sayin', Mr. Jamieson," said Kyle.

The coach looked around the hallway, seeming to direct his next comment to all the boys watching the exchange. "But basketball isn't just about skill and scoring points," he continued. "It's about teamwork and knowing when to pass the ball. It's understanding that five people get that ball to the hoop every time. Not just one." He shook his head solemnly. "You play like you're the only person on the court, Rafe. I don't need stars. I need a team." He turned to move down the hallway, then stopped and looked back. "If it's any consolation, you were on my first list, and I thought long and hard before cutting you. And if one of the boys I picked isn't able to play, I'll rethink my decision. Meanwhile, you've got some learning to do." He continued down the hallway, turned a corner, and was gone.

There was another awkward silence, and most of the boys gathered around the gymnasium bulletin board melted away. For a long moment, Rafe stood staring after Jamieson, an expression on his face unlike anything Jared had seen before. Then Rafe made a sound that might have been a laugh—or something else altogether—and strode off toward homeroom, Kyle and Pete trailing behind him.

Jared watched them go, all the while replaying in his head the scene that had just unfolded. He whistled under his breath, imagining another scene that would unfold later that day. When Rafe told his dad he hadn't made the team.

"Well?"

Jared turned to see Steve standing by the list, the smile on his face showing every one of his teeth. "Well, what?" Jared asked.

"How's it feel to be a Cougar?"

It took a moment for the question to hit home. "You *serious?*" Jared said, his voice little more than a croak. "I made the team?"

Steve's smile threatened to split his face in two. "We *both* did, buddy!"

* * *

The two friends were still crowing over their good fortune and slapping each other on the back when they arrived at the door of Mr. Keaton's classroom.

"I can't believe it!" Jared exclaimed for the tenth time. "We're Cougars!"

"I keep thinkin' I'm gonna wake up and Mom'll be yellin' for me to get ready for school," said Steve. "I keep pinchin' myself to make sure I ain't dreamin'."

Jared grinned. "Same here."

The warning bell rang, and Steve high-fived his friend once more. "See you at lunch, okay?" Then he was off, still shaking his head in disbelief.

Jared entered the classroom, making a conscious effort to keep from whistling. He'd spied Rafe across the room, muttering to Pete and Kyle, and he didn't want them to think he was rubbing it in about being picked for the team over them. As he made his way toward his seat, he passed Ellie, who had her nose buried in what looked to be a dictionary. Figures. But even her weirdness couldn't take the edge off his excitement. He couldn't wait to go one on one with Steve at lunch. Now that they were Cougars, they *really* had to practise.

"Hey, Jared."

Jared turned to see Rafe smiling at him.

"Congratulations."

Jared nodded, embarrassed by the attention. Usually Rafe didn't give him the time of day. "Thanks," he said.

Rafe turned as though to speak to Pete and Kyle, but his voice was loud enough for Jared to hear. "Hey, don't we get our math quizzes back today?"

Jared's exhilaration vanished, and he suppressed a groan. The math quiz. He'd forgotten all about it.

Well, so much for making the team. Once Jamieson got wind of his math mark, that would be the end of his career as a Cougar. The shortest on record.

Jared looked again at Rafe, who flashed him an even broader smile.

* * *

The morning seemed to pass in slow motion as Jared waited for math period to begin. Social studies, French, and language arts crawled by. Even recess brought him no relief. Although it was an unusually warm day for late October, he didn't go outside, but just sat in his seat and played with his pencil, doodling the word "Cougars" over and over again on his paper before drawing an X through all of them. When Mr. Keaton asked if he was feeling okay, Jared just shrugged and kept doodling and drawing Xs.

"I heard you made the team, Jared," said Mr. Keaton. "That's terrific!" When Jared didn't reply, the teacher continued, "Mr. Jamieson spoke to me about you this morning in the staff room. He was very impressed by what he saw."

Ordinarily, praise like that from the coach would have sent Jared into cartwheels. But he only shrugged. Just as Mr. Keaton was about to say something else, the bell rang and the rest of the students began pouring into the room.

When the class had taken out their math books, Mr. Keaton reached into his briefcase and pulled out a folder thick with papers. "I marked your math quizzes last night, and I'd planned to pass them back at the end of math—"

Loud groans from many of the students interrupted him.

The teacher grinned. "As I said, I had *planned* to pass them back at the end of math, but I think today I'll pass them back at the beginning."

Jared looked down at his "Cougar" doodles, drew a large X again through all of them, and crumpled the paper in his fist.

As usual, Mr. Keaton began by commenting on the

performance of the class in general before moving on to specific students. Although he never passed back tests or assignments in order of marks, he often singled out individuals who had done exceptionally well or showed real improvement. "Five people scored perfect marks," Mr. Keaton said. He called out their names and passed their quizzes back to them. Ellie, of course, was among them, as was Rafe, who was an excellent student overall and sometimes tied with Ellie for highest in math.

"There were three others," continued the teacher, "who scored second highest on the quiz, losing only one point for simple mistakes." He called out two names—Emily Richards and Bobby Hightower—and then the third.

A murmur floated over the rows, and Jared looked up. Everyone seemed to be looking at him. Including the teacher.

"Aren't you going to come get your quiz?" Mr. Keaton asked.

Jared turned around to look at Lisa Berringer, who sat directly behind him.

"Not me," Lisa said. "He means you."

Jared's mouth opened, closed, then opened again. "Me?" he finally managed to ask.

Mr. Keaton wore a smile similar to the one Jared had seen on Steve's face earlier that morning. "Yes, Jared. You." He held up Jared's quiz. "The only mistake you made was forgetting to write your final answer in a sentence. Everything else was correct."

His face burning, Jared pulled himself to his feet and walked the few steps to the teacher's desk. He took his paper and stared at it for a moment in disbelief.

The teacher patted him on the back. "Fantastic work, Jared. Keep it up, okay?"

Someone in the class said "Go, Jared!" and a couple of other students whistled raucously. Jared looked up to see broad smiles on almost everyone's faces, including Ellie's.

Only three people weren't smiling.

Kyle Wethers and Pete Johnson.

And Rafe Wells.

* * *

"This is *terrific!*" Steve exclaimed as he looked at Jared's quiz. The two boys were sitting in the school cafeteria, their chicken casserole untouched in the face of Jared's staggering accomplishment. "And second highest, too! Your mom is gonna *freak*."

Jared grinned. "I know. I can't wait to see her face when I show it to her."

"But what's best," said Steve, "is the pressure's off. No more worryin' about Keaton's academic probation. You're a Cougar for keeps!"

"Looks like it, don't it?" Jared agreed. "Mr. Keaton said this quiz will really help bring up my math mark, and just in time, with report cards coming out soon." He took the paper from his friend, folded it neatly, and slid it into his back pocket. "C'mon, let's go shoot some hoops. I'm too excited to eat."

Steve pushed his tray back and got up. "Just as well," he said, shaking his head at the food on his plate. "The Chicken Supreme has definitely seen better days. Like last Tuesday, maybe?"

Jared chuckled. The two friends picked up their trays and made their way toward the large aluminum rack on the other side of the cafeteria. After sorting their recyclables and depositing their trays, they headed down the hallway toward the basketball courts.

"Of course," Steve said as they pushed through the double doors into the bright sunshine, "every silver lining has a cloud."

Jared scanned the courts to see which of the two games in progress they could join. "Whaddya mean?" he asked.

Steve looked at him. "Don't you remember?"

"Remember what?"

"You said that once you found out you didn't make the team, you could quit the tutoring."

Jared stopped short.

Steve was obviously enjoying the moment. "And since

you *did* make the team, it kinda looks like you and Ellie Brejovic will be spendin' a *lot* 'a time together."

Groaning, Jared shook his head.

"Just think," Steve teased. "This could be the beginning of a beautiful friendship." He stretched out the word "beautiful," emphasizing each syllable.

Jared groaned again. Getting picked for the Cougars and scoring second highest on a math quiz suddenly didn't seem quite so terrific after all.

CHAPTER 12

"Well, if it isn't the conquering hero!" Jared's mother exclaimed as she met him at the door and wrapped her arms around him. In the kitchen behind her, Cal barked as if he understood exactly what all the commotion was about.

"Aw, Mom!" Jared peeled his mother off him and shot a worried glance toward the unfamiliar car in the driveway. He hadn't noticed anyone inside when he'd run past it, anxious to share his news with his mother, but maybe he hadn't looked closely enough.

But his mother was determined. She hugged him again and pulled him into the kitchen, showering him with kisses. Even Cal got a few slobbery licks in when his mom finally pulled away.

Jared was mystified. "How'd you find out?"

"I told her."

Jared turned to see Mr. Keaton standing in the doorway to the living room. He was holding a steaming mug of coffee and, somehow, he looked different than he usually did. It took Jared a moment to realize the teacher's tie was missing. On anyone else, the difference wouldn't have been noticeable, but on Mr. Keaton, who always wore perfectly coordinating tie, dress shirt, and slacks, it was almost like catching the man in his pyjamas. Jared gaped at him.

"Sorry, Jared," the teacher said. "I was so pleased with your performance on the quiz that I wanted to tell your mother in person." He noticed Jared looking at the coffee mug in his hand and flushed. "Ah . . . your mother . . . she offered . . ."

Jared's mother ushered them both into the living room. "Please, Mr. Keaton—"

"Call me Ron," the teacher said, and Jared saw him flush again. *Ron?* This was just too weird.

"Please," Jared's mother continued, and this time Jared saw *her* face grow pink, "sit down." Turning to Jared, she said, "Where is it?"

"Where's what?" Jared felt as if he'd suddenly stepped into a bizarre parallel universe—although all the faces were the same, the people wearing them were somehow different, somehow not the same people he'd seen earlier that day. Mr. Keaton in their living room? Without a tie? Drinking coffee?

"The quiz!" said his mother, settling herself on the sofa, across from the armchair where the teacher sat. She still wore her nurse's uniform, so Jared knew she hadn't been home long. Mr. Keaton—Jared couldn't possibly think of him as *Ron*—must have been waiting for her in the driveway. "I'd like to see it."

Jared reached into his pocket and pulled out the carefully folded paper, smoothed it out, and passed it to his mother.

She looked at it, then at him, then at the paper, then back at him as if she, too, found herself in that same bizarre universe and was now trying to recognize the person in front of her. "Oh, honey, this is amazing," she said, and Jared thought he could detect the beginnings of tears in her eyes.

"Aww, Mom," he repeated, suddenly desperate to change the subject. "So you heard about the other thing, too, huh?" he asked.

From across the room, Mr. Keaton cleared his throat, and Jared saw the teacher shake his head. "I thought you should tell her that news yourself," he said.

"Tell me what?" his mother asked, then her eyes widened. "The team list," she said softly. "It went up today, didn't it?" Her eyes widened even further. "Well?"

Jared beamed. "I made the cut! You're lookin' at a Cornwallis Cougar!"

Jared's mother leaped off the sofa and wrapped her arms around her son once more. "Jared! That's terrific! I'm so *proud* of you!"

This time, Jared gave in and let her hug him. It wasn't every day he got to be both a math marvel *and* a Cougar. No matter *how* weird this new universe was, he was pretty sure even in *it,* the odds of that happening again were next to impossible.

Mr. Keaton cleared his throat again. "Look, I should be going," he said as he stood up, being careful not to spill his coffee. Jared and his mother followed him into the kitchen.

"I can't tell you how happy I am to see such improvement in your math, Jared," the teacher said, setting the coffee mug on the counter. "I know Ellie's excellent one-on-one tutoring had a lot to do with it, but that alone wouldn't have done you much good if you hadn't put in the time and effort. You keep it up, okay? I'm looking forward to watching you play as a Cougar, but you need to keep working hard to make sure that continues to happen. Right?"

Jared nodded. "Right."

"It was nice to . . . ah . . . see you again, Ms. St. George," said Mr. Keaton.

"Please. Call me Terri."

"Terri." He said the word tentatively, held out his hand and shook hers. Jared noticed that he didn't release it right away, just kept holding her hand and looking at her. If possible, the teacher's face was even redder than before. He seemed about to say something when there was a knock on the door. Mr. Keaton started, stepping back as he finally let go.

Jared's mother went to the door and opened it. "Ellie!" she said, and beckoned the girl into the kitchen. Ellie stopped and smiled shyly when she saw the teacher. "Mr. Keaton dropped by to tell me what a great job Jared did on his math quiz. He says you deserve a lot of the credit."

Ellie flushed and looked down at her hands. "Thanks," she mumbled, "but Jared really worked hard during our sessions."

Jared's eyes widened at her comment. He hadn't *felt* like he'd worked hard. In fact, it felt like just the opposite—he'd complained constantly while she'd coaxed him to look at other examples, try different strategies, and make up his own problems. He thought he'd been a major pain in the butt. Yet here she was saying how hard he'd worked. "Nah," he said, "you really helped me understand it. When I was doin' the quiz yesterday, I thought about what you did with the noodles, and then the problem just sort of opened up in my head." Suddenly, he was aware of his mother and Mr. Keaton looking at him. "She did this thing with a box of Kraft Dinner," he told them. "It really helped me understand what perimeter and area and volume are."

Mr. Keaton laughed. "Ellie," he said, "you'll have to share your Kraft Dinner secret with me sometime."

Ellie looked up and smiled, a real ear-to-ear smile that showed teeth and dimples and, for the first time, Jared didn't see the third-row weirdo everyone made fun of.

CHAPTER 13

"So, one way to find patterns in a number sequence," Ellie explained during their session two days later, "is to subtract each pair of numbers and see if their differences are the same." She wrote some numbers on scrap paper lying on the kitchen table. "Or, if they're not the same, maybe their differences are connected in some way. Like these." She showed Jared the figures she'd written—1, 2, 4, 7, 11, 16, 22, and 29—and explained that although their differences weren't the same, the differences did follow a pattern. "So what would the next number in the sequence be?" she asked.

Jared looked at the list of numbers and said, "Thirty-seven?"

Ellie nodded. "How do you know?"

Jared raised his shoulders. "I just know," he said.

Ellie shook her head. "It's not enough to just know. You need to be able to explain *how* you know."

Jared pushed his chair back from the table. "Why? What's so important about number patterns anyway?" He picked up the list of number sequences that Mr. Keaton had given them as part of their homework, then scowled at the paper and shoved it aside. "This is stupid."

Ellie sighed and put her pencil down. "I don't think number patterns by themselves are all that important, either. But being able to *recognize* patterns is."

"Why?"

Ellie thought for a moment. "I think because it can help make you a better problem solver."

Jared wasn't convinced. "How?"

Ellie didn't say anything for another moment, then her eyes brightened. "Think of a basketball game. Let's say you noticed that every time a player on the opposite team got the ball, he always positioned himself in the same spot before he made a shot. What would you do?"

Jared didn't even pause. "I'd get there ahead of him and block him before he could take the shot."

Ellie smiled. "Right. You recognized a pattern and—"

"—and came up with a way to stop him," Jared finished, smiling.

"Right. It's the same with math problems. Say you notice a pattern in a problem—maybe you realize it's a lot like a problem you solved before. You can use the same strategy that worked the last time to solve the new problem. That way you save time. You don't keep repeating the same mistakes you made before."

Jared nodded slowly. "Okay."

"So how'd you get thirty-seven?" Ellie asked.

He grinned sheepishly. "Just a guess."

Ellie raised her eyebrows. "Well, it was a lucky one. The next number *is* thirty-seven. But can you tell me why?"

Jared reached for the paper and jotted down the differences between several pairs of numbers. "I don't get it," he said, scratching his head. "Oh, wait, I made a mistake." He erased a number, replaced it with another, and stared again at the list he'd made. Then his eyes widened. "I think I see it now," he said. "Each time the number got bigger, it was by one more than the last time. So I added eight to the last number to get thirty-seven. I'd have to add nine to thirty-seven to get the number after that."

"That's right," said Ellie, clearly pleased.

"And the rest of the homework is the same sorta thing?"

She nodded. "Pretty much. Don't be surprised, though, if you find one or two that don't really seem to follow a pattern. Mr. Keaton put a couple of tough ones in there to challenge us. You just have to think about what's happening to the numbers in the list. Ask yourself,

'Are they getting bigger or smaller?' and 'Do they get bigger or smaller in the same way?' It sometimes helps to think of each one as a puzzle. That's what I do, anyway." She glanced at her watch. "Time's up."

Jared looked at the clock and was surprised to see they'd been sitting at the kitchen table for over an hour. He got up and helped Ellie collect her things. As usual, she had lots of books in her bag, and not just on math. One had pictures of fish on the cover.

"Why do you carry so much stuff around?" Jared asked.

Ellie reddened. "You never know when you'll need something," she said.

"The whole 'be prepared' thing, huh?" said Jared.

"There are worse things than being prepared," she said, and Jared caught a defensive note in her voice.

"I didn't mean it was bad," he said. "I just wondered what you had in there."

Ellie looked at him for a long moment, as if trying to make up her mind about something.

"Jeez," Jared said, "forget I asked. I don't care what you've got in your stupid bag, anyway."

A shadow seemed to flicker over Ellie's face. "No, I'm sure you don't," she mumbled, hoisting the bag to her shoulder. She left without saying goodbye.

Jared stood looking out the window as she walked down the street, wondering how she could have gone from tutor to totally weird in seconds. Girls. Did anyone understand them?

He cleared the scrap paper off the table and took it to the wastebasket they used for dry trash. Lying on top of the trash was an envelope from a greeting card. That was strange. Bills and junk mail seemed to pour into their house by the bagful, but it was unusual for him or his mother to get something personal. The only family they had was his uncle, and Christmas was too far away for them to be hearing from him now. And both his and his mother's birthdays were in the spring.

Jared picked up the envelope and turned it over. Addressed to his mother, it had obviously been written by a man, the lettering heavy and square.

He thought about the last man who had sent his mother a greeting card, a blind date someone at work had fixed her up with during the summer. Jared had forgotten his name, but it didn't matter—he and his mom only ever referred to him as "DVD Guy." Part of the reason was that he repaired electronics at one of the big box home entertainment stores in the industrial park. The rest had to do with what happened the day after their date.

On their one and only evening out, Jared's mother happened to mention that her DVD sometimes skipped when it played rented movies. The following morning, the guy showed up at their door with two DVD players that he'd taken from the repair department where he worked. "Their owners didn't return to claim them," he said nonchalantly. "May as well go to someone who needs 'em." When Jared's mother—speechless until that point—commented that the machines probably belonged to the store now, he shrugged and said, "Who cares? I take stuff from there all the time. No one says anything." She had abruptly told him to take his DVD players and leave, and Jared still remembered how upset she'd been the rest of that day. "The guy probably steals clothes off corpses!" she had ranted.

The next day, a card arrived with an apology and a coupon for thirty percent off her next electronics repair service. She immediately threw both in the trash. And vowed never to go on another blind date.

Jared looked at the envelope in his hand. The postmark was smudged and the return address had been torn off. More weirdness. Why would his mother . . .

Jared shook his head and let the envelope fall back into the wastebasket. Females, it seemed, were just like math—impossible to figure out.

CHAPTER 14

"Get open!" Jared called as he dribbled the ball at half-court, his feet moving constantly as he dodged from side to side just out of reach of Mark Kowalski, the shirt who was guarding him. Jared scanned the bodies moving in and out of the key, shirts and skins weaving tangled patterns under the basket, then saw Steve break free of the group. Jared stepped back and Mark dove forward, reaching for the ball, just as Jared passed the ball over Mark's head to Steve, who caught it, spun, and leaped toward the basket. Although Steve was shorter than most of the Cougars, his legs were coiled springs that propelled him high above the others, allowing him to slam the ball down through the hoop.

A cheer rose from the handful of students watching

the practice from the bleachers lining the gymnasium. Coach Jamieson blew his whistle and, as if choreographed, the players dropped their arms simultaneously and moved as one to the centre of the gym, sitting in a circle around the coach.

"Nice work out there, Lewis. You, too, St. George." He nodded toward Mark. "Strong guarding, Kowalski. You never let up, kept on him right to the end. But he got the ball by you. Where'd you go wrong?"

Mark shook his head. "I dunno. I had my eye on the ball the whole time."

Jamieson nodded. "That's the problem. You were focused on the ball. You weren't watching his eyes. Players lie with their bodies, fake a pass with their arms, move their legs to make you think they're going left when they're really going right. But eyes tell us everything. St. George told you exactly what he was going to do before he did it. You just weren't watching."

"Sorry, Coach," Mark said.

Jamieson shook his head. "Don't be sorry. Be smart. *Play* smart." He looked at his watch. "Okay, two laps and then hit the showers."

Although every player wanted to groan, not one of them made a sound. No matter how gruelling the practice, Jamieson always wrung one last burst of energy from them. "You'll never know how strong you are if you don't push yourself," he'd told them their first afternoon practising as a team. At the time, Jared's knees were buckling and his arms felt like lead bars, but he'd run laps with the others and was surprised at how much more he could coax out of his weary body.

Halfway around the gym now, Jared felt the familiar click inside like the switch on a hidden reserve of strength, and he pushed himself harder until, at the end of the first lap, he was at the front of the group, with Mark Kowalski. The two teammates grinned at each other, put on one more burst of speed, and raced the final length of the gym shoulder to shoulder. A few of the remaining spectators cheered them on. Just as the runners pounded down the final few metres of the second lap, Jared saw Rafe standing by the bleachers, apart from the others. Rafe wasn't cheering. His hands were jammed in his pockets, his arms like exclamation points against his sides. But it wasn't his body language that spoke loudest to Jared. It was his eyes.

* * *

"Did y'see Rafe at the practice?" Steve asked later, as the two rode the bus home.

Jared nodded. "Was he there the whole time?"

Steve shook his head. "Just at the end. I heard his dad was meetin' with the principal after school."

Jared grimaced. "I thought he already met with Jamieson."

"He did," said Steve. "And accordin' to Keith, it was a real shoutin' match." Keith Baxter, one of the other seventh-grade players, had gone to see the coach after school about a brace for the knee he'd twisted during their first practice. He'd stood outside the gym office, waiting for Jamieson, and although the door was closed, he could hear the raised voices behind it clearly. "Keith said that Rafe's dad was pretty upset, yellin' about all the computers he'd donated to the school."

Jared had already heard all about it, but it continued to be a hot topic of conversation among the Cougars. "Do ya s'pose the principal will make Jamieson put Rafe on the team?"

Steve shrugged. "I dunno. Seems like that's the coach's decision, not the principal's."

"Yeah," Jared agreed. But he'd overheard Rafe telling some guys one day about how his dad and the principal went way back, how they'd known each other since they were in university together. Which was one of the reasons his dad had donated the computers to Cornwallis Middle School. That and because Rafe went there. He told Steve what he'd heard.

"Look," Steve said, "it don't matter *what* the principal does. Me and you are Cougars, right?"

"As long as I keep my marks up," Jared reminded him.

"Right. And after that quiz last week, you sure don't gotta worry about that."

Jared wasn't convinced. "We got a big math test comin' up. On all the stuff we been doin' since school started. It's worth a big chunk of our report card mark in November."

"Which is when basketball season starts," Steve observed.

"Right."

"So what? After all that extra work you been doin', buddy, you're gonna do fine."

"I hope so," Jared replied, but he wasn't so sure. He certainly seemed to understand the work much better since Ellie had begun tutoring him, but could he keep it up? And how much longer would she be tutoring him anyhow? She'd been putting in more than the required number of hours each week, so she couldn't be far from getting her extracurricular credit. What would happen then?

"So, you got another math session this afternoon, huh?" asked Steve.

"Yeah." Jared stared out the window at the blur of buildings and people they passed. Funny how things could be so clear one moment and so fuzzy the next. Like these sessions with Ellie.

"You ain't been complainin' about it as much," offered Steve.

Jared stared at him. "What's that s'posed to mean?"

"Nothin'. I just ain't heard you grumblin' like you used to."

Jared felt a heat work its way up the back of his neck. "You think I'm *enjoyin'* it?"

Steve snorted. "Yeah, like I'd think *that*." He hoisted his gym bag over his shoulder as the bus pulled up to their stop. "I'm just sayin' you surprised me. I gotta hand it to you. I know how much you can't stand Ellie Brejovic. Must be tough havin' to spend so much time with her."

Jared didn't say anything, just stood and followed his friend off the bus.

* * *

Waiting for Ellie to arrive, he thought again about what Steve had said. His friend was right. He *hadn't* been complaining as much about the sessions. But that didn't mean he was *enjoying* them. What he enjoyed was the time they saved him. After all, what wasn't there to like about getting help with homework that would have taken him a whole lot longer by himself than with Ellie?

No, you certainly couldn't say he was enjoying their time together. But yes, he liked how Ellie made math mean something, how she could take a question about probability or proportions and make it into something he cared about, like basketball or soccer. He liked how she didn't make him feel stupid when an answer was staring him right in the face and he couldn't see it. How she never lost her patience, how she seemed genuinely happy for him when he finally found his way through the maze that was his math homework. *That's* what he enjoyed.

Halfway though their session that day, though, he began to wonder if that was entirely true. Besides her knack for making math seem real, even interesting, she had a quirky sense of humour that reminded him of those old British television shows he sometimes watched on the Comedy Network. Most of the kids at school thought they were dumb, but he found them weirdly funny. Ellie's peculiar slant on things was much the same. He hadn't noticed that during their first few sessions together.

They finished a few minutes early and, rather than immediately packing up and saying goodbye, Jared found himself asking Ellie if she'd heard about class clown Jimmy Stoltz's latest practical joke on Mr. Grady, the head janitor. Jimmy told some of the boys in 6K how he had tied a pair of women's underwear—a lacy black thong, to be precise—to the end of the long-handled duster he'd found in the janitor's supply closet. Far from ambitious, Grady was well known for the careless way he worked. He was usually absorbed in some talk-radio program he listened to with a headset as he haphazardly cleaned his section of the building, and he'd been warned at least twice by the principal to improve his performance. Jared and the others who knew about Jimmy's prank were waiting to hear if Grady had even noticed the underwear.

It turned out that Ellie had first-hand news of the outcome. She'd stayed after school for a few minutes to update Mr. Keaton on her tutoring, and she'd passed the janitor on the way out. Earphones firmly in place, he had been lazily swiping the duster—and, of course, the thong—back and forth across the glass in the atrium. And with all that afternoon sunshine streaming in on him, he'd looked like he was performing onstage in a spotlight. Jared found Ellie's description of the moment hysterical, and it was only a coughing fit that brought an end to his laughter.

That had led to conversation about other people at school, like Ms. Curtis, the teacher of the class across the hall from theirs. "You know she has a huge crush on Mr. Keaton, don't you?" asked Ellie.

Jared was incredulous. "You're kiddin'. Ms. Curtis?"

"You've never seen?"

"Seen what?"

Ellie grinned. "How she always comes to Mr. Keaton when her whiteboard marker's dried up or she's low on printer paper."

Jared rolled his eyes. "Oh, right, all the signs of true love."

Ellie wagged her pencil at him. "It's not the *stuff*, Jared. It's the excuse it gives her to come to his room."

He wasn't convinced. "Teachers borrow from each other all the time."

"You haven't noticed how she leans over his desk and laughs at everything he says?"

Jared thought for a moment, and a memory of a recent recess surfaced: Ms. Curtis throwing her head back and laughing loudly at something Mr. Keaton had said about teaching fractions. He remembered thinking at the time how nothing about fractions could ever be *that* funny. Could Ellie be right? "Keaton don't seem to notice," he said. "Maybe he's married."

"Divorced. No kids."

Jared whistled under his breath. "Wow. You work as a private investigator when you aren't tutoring?"

It was Ellie's turn to laugh. "Nothing like that," she explained. "I was in the office once and overheard him asking the secretary about changing the bank account that the school board deposits his paycheque into. He told her he'd done it a couple years ago when he got divorced but he needed to do it again." She looked closely at Jared before continuing. "What was that like for you, Jared?"

"What was *what* like?"

She reddened and looked down at the table. "I can't believe I asked that. Sorry. It's none of my business."

Then he understood. "You wanna know about my mom's divorce."

"Really," she said looking up again, "you don't have to tell me."

"No, it's okay." Besides his mom, Steve was the only

person he'd talked to about it. No one else had ever asked. "I guess things started to go wrong after I was born. Maybe *because* I born."

Ellie looked at him, a pained expression on her face, and he smiled. "I guess some guys just aren't cut out to be dads. Mine wasn't. I don't remember him much." But he told her what he did remember—about the tall man with the big laugh who used to carry Jared on his shoulders so his head almost touched the ceiling. And about how the man started to laugh less and less and then, one day, left without even saying goodbye. They hadn't heard from him since. And didn't need to. His mother had built a life for the two of them that was just fine.

He stopped, surprised that he'd said so much. He thought of how awkward he'd felt talking to Samantha and Erica in the hallway that morning a couple weeks ago, and so instead listened to them chatter endlessly about fake fingernails. He'd never talked this much to a girl before. "What about you?" he asked. "It's just you and your dad, right?" He knew Ellie's mom had died, but he didn't know how.

She told him how her family had lived in Mostar, a wartorn city an hour's drive from Sarajevo, in Bosnia. Her mother had been leaving a bakery near their home when a car bomb exploded, instantly killing her and three other people. It was her dad who'd found Ellie's mother, had gone looking for her when she hadn't come home. Ellie, whose real name was Illyana, was only a baby when it happened. Immediately after the funeral, her father had applied to emigrate to Canada. He had a cousin already in Nova Scotia who sponsored him, which cut down the wait time. He couldn't leave Bosnia fast enough, couldn't bear the thought of maybe one day losing his daughter, too, and Canada seemed like a place where she could grow up safely.

But even now, her father didn't really feel *any* place was safe for her, which was why he'd always kept her close, why she was always with him at the deli, why he'd home-schooled her for the first few years rather than enrolling her in the public system. She'd learned to read when she was four, and books became her only companions. She was smart in book things, Ellie said, but not so smart when it came to kid things, being around people, making friends. Which was why her dad had finally decided to send her to public school the year before. She didn't think it had helped much. Even Felicity Flowers wasn't really a friend, just someone who sat with her on the playground sometimes because she liked the lunch Ellie's dad packed for her.

But she said none of this in a please-feel-sorry-for-me way, just answered his questions, told him what he wanted to know. Jared, though, felt humbled when he thought about how *his* father had *chosen* to leave while Ellie's mother had had the choice made *for* her—by someone she'd probably never even met.

Their conversation drifted to other topics. Jared asked Ellie about the music she liked to listen to, the type of movies she liked to watch, the food she liked to eat, and he was surprised they liked some of the same things. A *lot* of the same things, actually. He was even more surprised to glance at the clock and see that more than two hours had passed since Ellie had arrived.

When she saw the time, she nearly leaped from her chair. "I'm really sorry," she told him. "You probably have a ton of things to do."

"Not really," he began, but she continued to gather up her things in record time, apologizing twice more before she got her coat on and made it out the door.

This time as he watched through the window, he didn't see the Sherpa he'd imagined before. Sherpa mountaineers carry other people's loads up those slopes. Ellie carried a load all her own.

CHAPTER 15

"I'm home!" Jared called as he came in the back door, dropping his backpack and gym bag on the bench. He could hear the shower running.

Cal followed him inside and headed immediately for his dish, then gave Jared a look of disappointment when he found it empty. "You're gonna have to cut back, Cal," Jared said. "You're startin' to pork out in the hind end." The dog just stared at him.

"How was practice?" his mother called.

Jared poured himself a glass of orange juice and went to stand outside the bathroom door, taking gulps between play by plays of that afternoon's action. "I can't wait till the season starts," he said. "I wanna see how we do against another team."

He heard the water shut off and his mother pull back the shower curtain. In a moment, she came out into the hall in her bathrobe, towel-drying her hair. "The nurses on my floor can't wait, either," she said, grinning. "I've been bragging up my son, the Cougar, so much that a couple of them said they're coming to your first game if they're not working."

"Jeez, Mom," Jared said, "no pressure or anything." But he smiled in spite of himself. There were plenty of Cougars who were every bit as good as—in fact, better than—he was, but leave it to his mom to make him the team star.

"Ellie called," she told him, heading into her bedroom. "She said you'll have to go to *her* place this evening for your math session. Something about her dad being under the weather."

Jared thought about Ellie's father and wondered what bug could have affected such a hulk of a man. He was about to ask when his mother reappeared wearing a green dress he'd never seen before. And her best shoes. "Gee, you look nice," Jared told her.

"Hey, don't make it sound like such a surprise," she scoffed.

"I didn't mean—"

"I know, sweetheart. I'm just teasing," she said, putting on a pair of earrings. "I made up a plate and left it for you in the fridge. You just have to zap it in the microwave for two minutes."

"You already ate?" he asked, following her into the kitchen.

She looked at her reflection in the mirror by the back door. Seemingly satisfied, she turned. "No, as a matter of fact, I didn't. I have a date."

Jared's jaw dropped.

"I know," she said, "an old woman like me going on a date. Who'd have thought? But I've got my pension cheque with me, and I promise to take my walker." She picked up her purse. "Oh, Steve's mom said he could come over and watch some TV with you, but I told her you were going out for your math session."

Jared closed his mouth, then opened it again. "Who—?" He didn't even finish the question.

"Just a guy." She glanced at the clock and turned to kiss her son. "I'm going to meet him at the restaurant. I left the number on the counter." She opened the door. "Don't worry, I won't be out late. You know how us old folks need our rest."

* * *

Jared didn't know if he should ring the doorbell or knock. He didn't want to disturb Ellie's dad, but he wasn't sure anyone would hear him if he knocked. He was still making up his mind when the door opened.

"Hi," Ellie said. "I heard you on the stairs. Come in.

And don't mind Jacques." She pointed to a large iguana draped over the back of the sofa in a room off to the left. "Mrs. Finkleman, that's our housekeeper, she makes me put him in his cage when she comes to clean, but he wouldn't hurt a fly." She grinned. "Well, actually, he *would* hurt a fly. He loves 'em. But he wouldn't hurt people. He's too lazy."

Jared entered the foyer of the apartment above Brejovic's Deli. He'd wondered on the bus ride over what to expect, but he'd never in a million years have thought of an iguana. He wasn't surprised, however, when he saw plenty of pictures on the walls. Along the hallway she led him through were several photographs of an attractive young woman. "Your mother?" he asked. When she nodded, he said, "She was real pretty."

"My father says that I—" Ellie began, but then she stopped, embarrassed. "We can work in here," she said, leading him into a brightly lit kitchen. "Papa, this is Jared. The person I've been tutoring."

Ellie's father sat in a rocking chair in a room just off the kitchen, a small, glassed-in area that looked out over the tops of trees and the small yard below. A portable television sat on a table in the corner, its volume down low. The big man had his right foot up on a stool, and it was wrapped in an icepack. "I am remembering you from the deli," he said, his thick accent filling the room.

"Sorry to be not getting up." He nodded toward his foot.

"He sprained his ankle," Ellie explained, "climbing on the shelves in the cooler. Not using the stepladder like I've told him a hundred times." These last few words were directed sternly at her father.

"My Illyana," said Mr. Brejovic. "Much so smarter than her papa." He smiled broadly, and Jared recognized the same expression his mother often wore when she looked at Jared.

"Nice to meet you, Mr. Brejovic," said Jared.

"We'll be working at the kitchen table, Papa," Ellie said. "If you need anything—"

"I am being fine here," he said. "But excuse me, please, if I'm starting to snore. The pain pills the doctor is giving me—" He yawned.

"You should be in bed now," Ellie told him.

"Not before my news," he said.

Ellie turned to Jared. "He's hooked on news programs," she explained.

"There is so much to be learning about the world," her father said, yawning again. "You two go and be working, please. I am being fine."

Jared and Ellie sat down at the kitchen table. Even before Jared had opened his math binder to the homework Mr. Keaton had given them that day, he could hear

Mr. Brejovic snoring gently. Jared glanced at Ellie, who shook her head.

"There is so much to be learning about the world," she said.

Jared chuckled.

* * *

"So four-fifths plus a sixth is still less than one whole," said Jared.

"You're sure about that?" asked Ellie.

He frowned and was in mid-shrug when he caught himself. He smiled. "Yeah. I *am* sure."

Ellie gave him a thumbs-up. "You should be. You know this stuff now."

A loud, guttural snore filtered through the doorway off the kitchen, and Jared was suddenly conscious of the dark beyond the windows. "Gee, I should be going," he said. He got up from the table and slid his binder into his bag. He was glad he'd brought his warm jacket with him. The nights were a lot colder now.

Ellie followed him down the hallway. Zipping up his jacket, Jared turned to her. There was something he wanted to say, but he didn't know how. "I want—" He stopped.

"Did you forget something?" she asked, looking around.

He shook his head. "I really want to thank you for all

the help you've been givin' me," he said, embarrassment forcing the words out in a rush. His tongue felt like it was hinged on both ends, but he forged on. "You're real good at this, Ellie. You ever think 'a bein' a teacher?"

Now she was the one who flushed, embarrassed. She smiled shyly, nodding toward the photographs. "My mother was a teacher," she said quietly. She seemed about to say something else, but stopped.

"So you're gonna follow after her?" he asked.

She shrugged. "I like it, but it's not what I think I want to do."

Jared was surprised. "What's that?" he asked.

She looked down. "You'll just laugh."

"No, really," he said. "What is it?"

She looked at him for a moment, as if deciding something. "Do you have time to look at something?" she asked.

He nodded. "Sure."

Ellie led him into the room where the iguana still lay sprawled on the back of the sofa and through a doorway beyond. "Wow!" he said, frozen in mid-step, his eyes widening.

On three sides of the room were the largest aquariums he had ever seen, not counting the enormous tanks at the Fisheries Museum in Lunenburg, where he'd gone on a class trip when he was in grade four. Although the curtains were drawn, the room was far from dark, lit softly by the light cast from the aquariums' underwater lamps.

"Wow," Jared repeated as he stared at the illuminated fish and plant life. "Can I look?" But he didn't wait for an answer, his feet drawn like magnets to the aquatic displays. "Those are sailfin mollies," he said, his voice filled with awe as he pointed at several bulb-eyed creatures. "And look at the size of that pleco! Jeez, it must be half as long as my arm. You musta had him *forever!*"

"You know a lot about fish," Ellie said. He could hear the surprise in her voice, but she seemed pleased that Jared had noticed. "This guy was my first," she said, pointing at the pleco. "All the others in my first aquarium died. I didn't know how to take care of them, but this one survived. He's a tough one."

"What's his name?" he asked.

"Calypso," she replied.

"After Cousteau's ship." It was an observation, not a question.

Now it was her eyes that resembled those of the mollies. "How'd you *know* that?"

Jared knelt on the floor in front of one of the aquariums, never taking his eyes off the spectacular rainbowfish and gouramis inside. "That's my dog's name. I call him Cal, for short. I named him after Jacques Cousteau's boat that he used to explore—" He suddenly stopped, turning toward her with a wide grin on his face. "Jacques? You named your *lizard* after him?"

Ellie laughed. "Weird, I know—"

Jared cut her off. "Not weird at all. I think it's cool." His gaze wandered back to the tanks. "I always wanted an aquarium, but Mom said a dog was too much already in our small place. If she'd got me one, though, I'd have named my fish after people like Cousteau. Divers, people who explore the oceans . . ." He trailed off.

"How d'you know all this stuff?" Ellie asked.

Jared stood up, his eyes lingering on the aquariums. "You wouldn't believe me," he said softly.

"Sure I would. Tell me."

He turned to face her. "You promise you won't laugh?"

"I promise."

"When I was in grade four, our teacher did an oceans theme. Dolphins, sharks, sea turtles, stuff like that. She showed us one of Jacques Cousteau's underwater films—*The Silent World*—and ever since then I've wanted to be a marine biologist."

Her sudden laughter surprised him. Reddening, he looked down at the floor. He'd been an idiot to tell her.

"Sorry," she said, "I'm not laughing at you." When he didn't look up, she continued, "Really, I'm not. It's just that I want to be a marine biologist, too!"

Jared's jaw dropped. "No way!"

"Really," she said. "Since I was old enough to know what one was." Now it was Ellie's turn to look down and, when she spoke again, Jared had to strain to hear her words. "You know I don't really fit in," she said. "I guess I've spent my whole life on the outside of things." Jared expected her voice to trail off altogether, but instead, it became stronger. "I've gotten good at watching people, seeing the way they act, even figuring out why they do the things they do." She knelt by the nearest aquarium and peered through the glass, gently tracing with her fingertips the languid movement of a rainbowfish. "So when I first read about marine biologists, I decided that's what I wanted to be. I knew I'd be good at it, studying creatures underwater." She paused for a moment, and Jared heard her swallow before she continued. "A person couldn't be alone in the ocean when there's all that life around you."

Jared didn't know what to say. He thought of all the times he'd seen Ellie with a book in her hand and just assumed she was reading. Had she been watching the activity around her all those times? All alone on the outside looking in?

Still watching the movements of the fish, Ellie remarked, "You know, I would've thought you wanted to be a professional basketball player."

Jared nodded. "Me and my buddy Steve, we sometimes talk about that, imagine what it would be like. But only a few players ever make pro. Besides, it's what I do for fun. I think I'll always play basketball, no matter where I end up, but I think makin' it a job would ruin it, you know?" What did Ellie do for fun, he wondered. Was fun even something she ever had? Jared tried to change the subject. "I think it'd be cool to study sea life for a living. I watch those underwater shows on the Discovery Channel all the time. I saw one last week about creatures that live really deep in the ocean. There was this one fish that even makes its own light."

"I saw that, too," Ellie said. "The one about the lanternfish."

"Yeah. Amazin', huh?"

Ellie stood up. "Did you see the one about the Great Barrier Reef in Australia?"

"Twice," said Jared. "The part about the sharks was the best!"

They talked animatedly about how the divers protected themselves from the great whites and what it must be like to see one of those predators up close. Ellie was in the middle of telling him about a book she'd borrowed from the library about sharks when she paused. "Jared," she said after a moment, "why'd you think I'd laugh at you wanting to be a marine biologist?"

He looked down again, self-conscious. "The math."

"What d'you mean?"

"You need tons of maths and sciences to become one. My mom told me."

She nodded slowly. "You and the math thing," she said.

"Yeah. Me and the math thing." He grimaced. "Look, you won't tell anybody about this, will you? I mean, my mom knows, but I've never told anyone else. Not even Steve. It'd be like a blind guy sayin' he wanted to be a drivin' instructor." He managed a wry smile.

"Jared," Ellie said, "I think you can do anything you put your mind to."

He just shrugged.

"I mean it," she said. "Look at what you've done so far."

"But that's only because of you," he said.

She frowned. "Does Mr. Jamieson take the credit when you sink a shot?"

Jared blinked. "That's different."

"How's it different? He shows you how to do it and you do it. I haven't been doing your assignments and quizzes for you, have I? I showed you some things, but you did the rest yourself. Not me."

Jared felt embarrassed all over again. "Well, thanks . . ." he began.

"Don't thank *me,*" Ellie said. "Just know that you can do this math. The marine biology thing, too, I bet. Really."

* * *

Waiting at the bus stop to go home, Jared replayed his and Ellie's conversation over and over in his head. Sure, it was easy for Ellie to say he could do whatever he wanted, but she wasn't inside his head. He knew better. And that bit about becoming a marine biologist? Right. He couldn't even see beyond Wednesday, when they would write the big math test. The test that would decide for sure if he'd be playing the season with the Cougars.

He tugged his coat collar up against the cold and peered down the street for the familiar lights of the Metro Transit bus. But except for the streetlamps, all he could see was darkness.

CHAPTER 16

"And there were four people who handed in exemplary work," said Mr. Keaton as he passed back their math assignments. "Kristie, Jared, Ellie, and Rafe. Great graphs, people."

Rafe was the last one to collect his work from the teacher. He took the long route back to his seat, passing by Jared's desk. "You're turning into a real brainer, Jared," he said, his voice low. Jared was pretty sure it wasn't meant as a compliment, though. Maybe it had something to do with the hard-edged smile on Rafe's face. Or the way he crinkled his paper in his hands as he walked by.

Jared looked down at the assignment Mr. Keaton had returned to him and read the comment the teacher had written. *Outstanding work, Jared. You definitely know what you are doing here. Keep it up!* Was he really turning into a brainer? Or was he just fooling everybody, including himself?

The momentary rush of pleasure he felt was short-lived. Mr. Keaton began discussing the term test they would be writing the next day, how it would consist of various parts to reflect the topics and strategies they had been practising in math so far. Some sections of the test would be paper-and-pencil figuring, some sections would involve mental math and estimating, and some sections would require them to use manipulative materials such as the base ten blocks, Fraction Factory pieces, and two-colour counters they had been working with since the beginning of the school year. Jared listened to the teacher's explanation with a growing sense of unease, and even the terrific mark he'd just received on the graphing assignment did not keep the ball of lead from forming in his stomach, didn't keep it from growing and rolling around inside, knocking against the wall of his chest. Surely that wasn't his heart hammering in there. Nothing short of heavy metal could pound so loudly against his ribs.

Jared gripped the edge of his desk, pressing his fingers against the smooth, cool surface to remind himself that he was sitting in a classroom, not facing a firing squad. He tried to think of other things, things not involving schoolwork. Like what was going on with his mother, for example. He'd arrived home from Ellie's last night and found his mother watching television, some ridiculous reality TV program where ex-partners lived together in a sealed warehouse, their actions and conversations recorded and played back over and over so viewers first got to listen to them talk and then, on top of that, got to listen to them talk about what they talked about. His mother ordinarily hated shows like that—she usually made fun of the people on the screen, telling them what idiots they were, how they should get real lives and stop their non-stop whining on TV. But this time she'd been glued to the TV when he came in, actually listening to what the show's participants were saying.

Jared had asked her right off about her date, but her response was vague. "It was nice," she'd said absent-mindedly, her eyes returning to the screen. Come to think of it now, though, he wondered if maybe she'd just been pretending to be interested in the program so she wouldn't have to talk to him about her evening. When he'd asked her who her date was, she'd just shrugged off the question and pointed at the television—in other words, *Don't interrupt me.*

He wondered who the man was. His mother hadn't dated since DVD Guy. Oh, sure, she'd gone out with people from work, but those didn't really qualify as dates, more like friends unwinding, having a good time together. Jared thought for a minute. Hadn't she mentioned that Jerry guy from the hospital a few times? No, Jared didn't really think there was anything going on there. After all, what future could there be for a couple named Terri and Jerry? Sounded more like cartoon characters than people in a regular relationship. Of course, after watching a few minutes of that dumb reality TV show, who could be sure *what* a regular relationship was?

But then he remembered the envelope he'd found in the trash, the one she'd torn the return address off. If she *was* seeing someone, why keep it a secret? Why would she not want him to know who it was?

Jared had tried to talk to Steve about it on the way to school, but Steve had misunderstood, told Jared he was just being jealous and should butt out.

"I'm not jealous," Jared objected. "I don't care if my mom has a guy in her life." After all, her divorce had been finalized years ago, so there wasn't much chance of her getting back with the tall guy. Jared didn't even think of that person as his dad. Too much time had passed, too much of their lives had gone on without him. Besides, ex-partners weren't exactly good choices for—

Jared froze. He thought again about the program his mother had sat watching, pretending to be mesmerized by it. Or maybe not pretending at all. The show was about people and their ex-partners. Ex-husbands and ex-wives getting back together. Jared tried to shake away the prickle he felt race up his spine. *Ex-husbands.* It couldn't be. Could it?

Suddenly, it wasn't just math that was confusing.

* * *

"You okay?"

Jared looked up from his lunch tray to see Ellie standing by his table, looking more than a little out of place.

"All right if I sit down?" she asked softly.

Jared glanced around, wondering who else was still in the cafeteria. Most of his friends had already eaten and left, like Steve, whose dad had picked him up and taken him to the dentist. Jared had just been sitting there lost in thought again, puzzling over his mother's mystery date. "Uh, sure," he said. He looked down to see he'd barely touched his sloppy joe. Now *there* was a name that said it all.

Ellie sat in the seat across from Jared. He noticed she'd made the more sensible choice of tomato soup and crackers. How could they go wrong with soup? "You feeling all right?" she asked.

Jared raised his eyebrows. "Me? Why?"

Ellie dragged a cracker through her soup. The liquid reminded Jared of red paint. Or blood. Maybe there *was* a way to ruin tomato soup, after all.

"You've been staring at your food for the last five

minutes," she offered quietly. She nodded toward the table across from them. "I was sitting over there watching you."

Jared thought of her comment last night about watching people. What had she said? *I've spent my whole life on the outside of things.* He thought of her sitting at the other table looking at him, thought about how tough it must have been for her to pick up her tray and come over. Maybe almost as tough as writing a math test was for him. He didn't know what to say. He looked down, grimaced, and pointed to his plate. "Sloppy joes. They're not just for breakfast any more."

Ellie grinned and raised her soggy cracker, but it fell apart in mid-bite, half of it sliding down her chin and onto her shirt. "Oh . . ." she sputtered. "I probably look like something from a bad horror movie."

"Ever hear of *Attack of the Killer Tomatoes*?" Jared asked. He and Steve had rented the movie half a dozen times, hooting at the film's campy horror. "You're victim twelve." He offered her his untouched napkin.

"Really, though," she continued after dipping the napkin in her glass of water and blotting the soup off her shirt, "you okay? You looked worried about something."

"Not worried," he said. "Just . . . confused, I guess."

She sighed. "Remember, you just have to read the problems over two or three times first. Don't jump in till you're sure you—"

Jared laughed. "Believe it or not, for once I wasn't talkin' about math."

"What then?"

He looked at her across the table, and for the first time he noticed that Ellie had blue eyes. Not the kind of washed-out blue you see on most people, the blue that looks like it wants to be something else—gray, maybe, or green. No, *really* blue, the kind you see in travel ads where people splash around in water that smacks you in the face with its blueness. Like you'd just seen blue for the very first time and didn't know what you'd been missing. *That* kind of blue.

"Well, isn't this sweet," drawled a voice behind them.

Jared turned around to see Rafe standing with Kyle and Pete, the three of them grinning like the idiots he'd seen on that program last night. The Cornwallis Middle School version of reality TV. Without the cameras. "Hey, guys," Jared said. He didn't know why he felt foolish.

And then, of course, he did.

"I *thought* you must've been getting help with your math, Jared," Rafe said, looking at Ellie, "but I didn't know who from." He turned again to Jared. "How do you do it, anyway? Borrow brain cells? Ellie's sure got a few million to spare."

Jared looked at Ellie, who was staring at her tray. Her face resembled his sloppy joe. Shapeless. He didn't have to imagine what his own face looked like. *Red as berries,* his mother used to say when he got embarrassed. Redder than that, he thought. Blood red? No. Tomato soup red.

"You guys spend a lot 'a late nights together?" Kyle asked. "Doin' the studyin' thing, I mean?" He snickered and, behind him, Pete whistled. The long, low sound set Jared's teeth on edge.

Jared got to his feet. "Funny, guys."

Rafe shook his head. "Not us, Jared," he said. "*You*. All this time I thought you were actually learning this stuff, but the joke's on me. I should've known. The day Jared St. George *really* starts making hundreds in math is the day I start checking my underwear for diamonds."

"What are you *talkin'* about?" Jared demanded, his embarrassment flaring into annoyance.

"The assignments are one thing," Rafe said. "Anybody can copy those easy enough. But how do you do it with tests and quizzes? Mirrors? Or does Ellie here just slip you the answers?" He turned and smiled at her, but there was no warmth in his face. "You're such a brainer, you could do *two* tests in the time most of us take to do one." His eyes widened. "Is *that* how you do it? You do your test *and* his? Clever!"

Ellie slid her chair back and got up. "You guys are such losers."

"What *I* want to know," Rafe continued, "is what *you*

get out of it, Ellie. Sure, Jared gets to be a Cougar." A coldness crept into his voice. "But what floats *your* boat? Jared do any extra special favours for *you?*"

Behind him, Pete and Kyle hooted, and Jared could see they'd attracted the attention of several other students sitting nearby.

"You're a pig," Ellie said. Her voice was low and even, audible only to Jared and Rafe and his posse. But there was no mistaking its intensity.

"Oink, oink," said Pete. He elbowed Kyle, who began echoing the animal noises.

"Guys," said Jared, "this is stupid—"

"You're the stupid one, Jared, if you think you can go on cheating just so you get to be a Cougar."

"I have *not* been *cheatin'!*"

Behind him, Kyle made wet noises with his lips. "Either that or you been spendin' a lot 'a time with Smelly Ellie. Doin' the *test-takin' tango!*" The last few words sprayed from his lips, lost in a loud guffaw as he bent double, Pete slapping him on the back.

Even his mother wouldn't have used "red as berries" to describe his face now, Jared thought. It was stove-hot. Around him, several others in the cafeteria had begun to point and laugh. Jared's ears were pounding as the blood rushed to his head, but he could still make out a few giggled comments, like "Smelly Ellie and Jared St.

George!" and "Who would've thought *those* two!" He turned in the direction of the comments and saw Samantha and Erica wide-eyed and talking animatedly behind their hands.

He looked down at his sloppy joe, wanted to scoop it up and ram every bit of it down all their throats. He looked at Ellie, who was looking at him, and suddenly he wanted to ram some sloppy joe down *her* throat, too. This was all *her* fault! He hadn't wanted anything to *do* with her in the first place. And *now* look what was happening.

His face a furnace, he dug down deep for a way out, pawed over possibilities, rejected each of them, and then realized what he had to do. He turned away from Ellie. Forcing a grin, he shrugged. "You guys ain't gonna tell Keaton I cheated, are ya?" he asked softly.

Rafe's face flooded with triumph. "So I was right!" He looked at Pete and Kyle. "We aren't snitches, *are* we, guys?"

The boys behind him murmured agreement, their faces reflecting surprise at Jared's admission.

"Jared," Rafe continued, his voice low, "we've all cheated on tests before. Who hasn't?" He narrowed his eyes. "But it stops now, right?" It wasn't a question. "You just tell Keaton you need to change seats so you can see better or something. No more getting help from *her*, okay?"

Jared nodded. He couldn't bring himself to look at Ellie.

Rafe cocked his head and grinned. "Too bad the big math test is tomorrow. Right, guys?"

Pete and Kyle snorted. "Yeah, Jared. Too bad."

Rafe made ball-handling motions, then momentarily dribbled an invisible basketball before sinking it in an imaginary basket above Jared's head. "And don't worry about your Cougars uniform. Keep it. My old man says he's gonna get one specially made for me." He nodded to the others. "C'mon, guys. Let's go."

The three moved off, several pairs of eyes watching them go. Jared turned to look at Ellie. But she was gone.

* * *

Jared sat by the outdoor courts for the rest of the lunch break, watching some eighth-graders play three on three. Watching them but not seeing a single play, his mind returning again and again to that moment in the cafeteria. He'd worn a thin jacket that day and he shivered in the chilly October air, but it somehow seemed right that he was cold. Besides, he didn't feel like going inside.

When the bell rang and Jared finally returned to the classroom, he didn't have to ask Mr. Keaton to change his seat. Ellie had already changed hers. She sat in the far right row in the second seat from the front, her face buried in a book. She didn't look up at Jared when he came in, just kept staring at the pages in front of her. He could tell, though, that she wasn't really reading. Her eyes weren't moving.

The afternoon seemed five days long, and a film on personal hygiene only made it drag more slowly. Even class clown Jimmy Stoltz couldn't seem to muster up enough energy to make fun of the actors the filmmaker had hired to act as sixth-grade students. One "girl" had to be at least twenty years old, and two of the "boys" looked like they shaved on a regular basis. Even reality TV was better than that.

Basketball practice hadn't been much better. Steve watched from the bench—Coach Jamieson wouldn't let him play with his mouth still frozen from his visit to the dentist—but even from the sidelines it wasn't hard for Steve to see that something was wrong with his friend. "Get in the *game,* man!" he hissed when Jared ran past. "Jamieson ain't impressed." And why *would* he be? Jared fumbled pass after pass, missed easy layups, didn't sink a single foul shot.

"What's up?" Steve asked him on the bus ride home.

Jared started to tell him, but the words wouldn't form in his throat. "Just tired, I guess," he said finally. Somehow it was easier to let his friend think he was a slacker than a world-class jerk.

Steve scowled. "We got our first game of the season tomorrow afternoon, and it's like you were *sleepwalkin'* out there."

For a moment, Jared wished he *had* been sleepwalking, wished that the whole day had been just a bad dream and he'd wake up from it soon. But sitting there, feeling the bus jostle under him, he knew he was wide awake. He had to be. No nightmare had ever made him feel this bad.

CHAPTER 17

Jared sat staring at the jumble of words and numbers on the paper in front of him. He wrote down a few figures but erased them almost immediately. He looked at the paper again, jotted down some more numbers, then scrawled an X through them and crumpled the paper in his fist. He might as well be studying Egyptian hieroglyphs. He tossed the ball of paper into the wastebasket, but it was already overflowing and the paper tumbled to the floor.

"Having trouble, slugger?" Jared's mother asked as she came into the kitchen and opened the fridge door. Their new refrigerator didn't match the stove, but it had been on sale for forty percent off and the Sears payment plan offered zero percent interest for one year. Even a math moron like himself could understand the value of zero percent.

Jared's mother poured herself a glass of orange juice and came to stand beside him. "What's this?"

Jared sighed. "The math review Mr. Keaton gave us. It's supposed to help prepare us for the test tomorrow." He slouched in the chair.

She squeezed his shoulder. "Listen, buddy, that test won't be any harder than the quizzes you've been writing, just longer. Remember how well you've been doing on those, right?"

Jared put his head in his hands. "This ain't the same."

"*Isn't* the same."

"It *isn't*," Jared said, defeat in his voice. "There's too much stuff. It's too much to remember."

His mother squeezed his shoulder again. "You're getting yourself all worked up over nothing."

He gave her a blank look. "That's easy for *you* to say."

Jared's mother smiled sympathetically. "You're right. Most of this doesn't look *anything* like the stuff I did when I was your age."

"*Big* help, Mom," Jared muttered. He pulled himself up in his chair and turned to the review sheet once more.

His mother watched as he made a few more half-hearted attempts at the work before letting his pencil fall to the table. "Why don't you call Ellie?" she asked. "I bet she could help you sort this out."

Jared shook his head. "I don't think so."

"Why not? She's helped you before."

Jared turned to his mother and opened his mouth, but nothing came out. For a moment, he thought about all the ways he could answer that question, but he knew he didn't have the words to make her understand. "I need to do this myself," he said finally. That was, he knew, the only explanation she'd accept.

"Okay, buddy," she said. "Just don't beat yourself up over it, okay?" She ran her hand through his blond hair. "You're gonna do fine," she said, then wandered back into the living room with her orange juice.

Yeah, he thought, *I'm gonna do fine*. He reached out and grasped the pencil between his fingers, his thumbs pushing it into a shallow curve. He wondered how much pressure the pencil could take before it snapped. He pressed on it even harder for a moment, then released it. No sense breaking it. He'd already ruined enough that day.

For what seemed the thousandth time, he replayed the scene in the cafeteria in his mind, saw himself do what he did. Heard himself say what he said. That he'd been cheating.

He guessed he should be worried about what Rafe might do now. The principal took a hard line with cheaters—kids who got caught ended up with as many after-school detentions as it took for them to redo everything they'd cheated on, and they still got zero for the work. If Rafe went to the principal with Jared's "confession," he'd likely be in detention until mid-November. Worse, all those zeros for the tests and assignments he'd been doing would bury his math mark. No way would Jared pass the year.

But for some reason, he wasn't really worried about Rafe Wells. After all, Rafe was pretty sure he'd be getting what he wanted most—Jared's place on the team. And, looking at the unfinished math review spread over the kitchen table, Jared was pretty sure Rafe would, too.

Jared glanced at the cordless phone on the table and, for the umpteenth time, considered calling Ellie and telling her he was sorry.

But there was nothing he could say that would make a difference. To either of them.

CHAPTER 18

The buzzer sounded, and Jared jogged dispiritedly toward the bench. Halftime already, and he had barely seen any court time. And for good reason. Although he'd started in all their practices, he hadn't been first on the floor today. Coach Jamieson was clearly still annoyed with him for his lacklustre performance during practice the day before. And when the coach had finally put him on toward the end of the first half, Jared hadn't played much better. He'd repeatedly allowed the player he was guarding to slip by him, and all but one of Jared's shots had bounced off the rim. The one that didn't was an air ball.

The coach was livid. Taking the team into the locker room, he pointed out the things they'd been doing right: most of the guys had played hard, handled the ball well, made some strong drives to the basket. Steve, in particular, was responsible for sixteen of the points on the board. But the Gators were beating them to the ball, out-thinking them on defence, suckering them into fouling out.

"But that's not the worst of it," he snarled. The Cougars had seen their coach annoyed during practices, but they'd never heard this particular tone. "The worst is when players let their team down, when they just don't have the guts to get the job done." Jared didn't need to guess whom Jamieson was talking about. And if anyone else hadn't been sure, Jamieson left no doubts in their minds when he sent the team out to the bench but told Jared to stay behind.

It wasn't until the last player had left the locker room that the coach spoke. "St. George," he said. Jared would have preferred if Jamieson had continued to snarl. But his voice was filled with disappointment. "I don't know what's been going on with you the last couple of days, but you're not the player I saw during tryouts. Or the player who's been showing up at practice giving a hundred percent from first to last. I don't know *who* this person in front of me is." He shook his head. "I don't often break my rule about not picking grade six students for the team. This time I'm sorry I did." He turned to leave.

Jamieson's words were like razors, and Jared felt shame burn his face. More than anything, he wanted to explain. He owed the coach that much.

"Coach?" he said.

Jamieson looked back, his body poised in mid-stride.

Jared knew he had only a few seconds to make the coach understand. "You're right. My head hasn't been in the game."

The coach snorted. "Your head hasn't been in the *building!*" But he wasn't walking away. That, at least, was something.

"I've had some trouble with—"

The coach cut him off. "We've all got problems, St. George. But problems don't belong on the court. Basketball does. You're letting people down. And I don't just mean the team. Your friends are out there. Your *mother's* out there. But even worse," he said, his voice softening, "you're letting *yourself* down."

Jared looked at the floor, fought the fist-sized lump in his throat that threatened to crowd out his next words. "I can do it, Coach. Give me another chance. Please."

Jamieson gazed at him for a moment, and from behind him came the blast of the referee's whistle signalling the end of halftime. "I *know* you can do it. You proved that to me in every practice. The question is, do you *want* to?"

This time Jared did not hesitate. "Yes, sir."

The coach put his hand on the boy's shoulder. "Then *do* it."

Jared took a long swallow from his water bottle and then made his way out to the bench. Jamieson was right.

He was letting everyone down. He couldn't be thinking about Rafe or Ellie or Mr. Keaton or any of that stuff. Not even the math test he'd written only two hours earlier.

If he *did* think about it, he'd know this was his last time on the court as a Cougar. Because he knew he'd failed the test. And not just failed it. Failed it miserably. He'd left whole sections unanswered. And what he *had* done, he'd mostly guessed at. He'd forgotten everything he knew. Or maybe he hadn't known it in the first place. It was Ellie who had somehow convinced him that he could actually do the stuff, but he'd known all along that he was an idiot when it came to math. He'd just forgotten that sad fact for a while. Looking around Mr. Keaton's classroom at everyone bent over their tests, he'd watched their pencils flying over their papers, proving to the teacher how much they knew.

Well, he'd certainly proven *that* all right. He'd seen it in Mr. Keaton's eyes when he passed in his test. The teacher had flipped through it quickly, had seen all the empty spaces, the half-attempts, the Xs Jared had drawn through his work. He'd hated the look he had seen on Mr. Keaton's face. It was the same look Ellie had worn in the cafeteria.

Yes, he had let them both down, but he wasn't about to let the team down now. If this was going to be his last game as a Cougar, then people would remember it for the right reasons. He was going to play some basketball.

He listened as the coach began to reel off the names of the starters for the second half.

His name was first.

* * *

Jared mopped the sweat off his forehead with the bottom of his jersey as the team gathered around Mr. Jamieson in the final timeout. The coach was not the same person they'd followed into the locker room at halftime. This man was animated and overflowing with praise. Two minutes left in the second half, and the score was 82–79 for the Granville Gators.

"You've brought her back, boys," he said. "We were down nineteen points at the beginning of the second half, and now it's anyone's game. You can *do* this!" He knelt over his clipboard, quickly sketching a variation of a play they'd tried several times during practice. The team listened closely as he described the action that would unfold. In what seemed like no time, the referee's whistle blew and the team huddled for a final Cougar cheer.

Just before Jared jogged back onto the court, the coach gripped his shoulder. "Jared, about what I said before. I'm glad I broke my rule." He flashed Jared a thumbs-up as the players ran out on the floor.

"*Go*, Cougars! Wooo-*hooo!*"

Jared turned to see his mother and two of her friends from work clapping and cheering, and he couldn't help but grin. His mom would have no voice tomorrow.

A couple of seats over from his mother sat Mr. Keaton. The teacher was cheering, too. Not as loudly as his mom, of course, but loudly nonetheless. And he'd brought one of those goofy horns that made a blatting sound, like a cow with indigestion. Jared's grin grew bigger. He wouldn't have pegged Keaton as a goofy-horn kind of guy.

The referee gave one of the Gators the ball for the throw-in, and Jared saw Steve become a flurry of movement as the Gator tried to pass the ball to a teammate. When he finally attempted the pass, it deflected off Steve's waving hand and was caught by Keith Baxter, who passed it to Mark Kowalski. Mark drove toward the corner and faked a shot to the basket, instead passing it to Jared, who twisted, leaped, and slammed the ball home. The Cougar fans went wild.

Gators 82, Cougars 81.

Fifty-two seconds on the clock, and the Gators came back strong.

. . . Fifty-one, fifty, forty-nine . . .

The Gators dazzled the spectators—Gator fans and Cougar fans alike—with their footwork and ball-handling. Chest passes, bounce passes, even blind passes moved the ball slowly but surely up the court.

. . . Thirty-eight, thirty-seven, thirty-six . . .

Then one of the Gators took a gamble and drove toward the Cougar hoop, tossing the ball in a long arc toward the basket. It banked off the backboard and ringed the hoop twice before dropping down—

No! Airborne on his powerful legs, Steve swiped at the ball, knocking it out of bounds. The whistle blew and, with twenty-four seconds remaining on the clock, the referee gave the Gators the ball for the throw-in.

Despite a strong full-court press, the ball ended up in Gator hands and, just as the coach had predicted, the visiting team began a keepaway game, trying to run out the seconds. The ball criss-crossed the court from Gator to Gator, avoiding Cougar hands.

. . . fourteen, thirteen, twelve . . .

Exhausted and frustrated, Keith fouled a Gator from behind and the Cougar fans, who had been on their feet, sank back into their seats, many with their heads in their hands. The players positioned themselves for the foul shot, and Jared, glancing up at his mother, saw her crossing her fingers.

The Gator missed his first shot. But made the second. A collective groan rose from the Cougar supporters.

Gators 83, Cougars 81.

The referee handed Mark the ball for the throw-in. Mark passed it to Jared, the seconds on the clock ticking down.

. . . eleven, ten, nine . . .

Jared raced toward the far hoop, but two Gator defencemen blocked his run. His eyes scanned the court for someone to pass to. Cougars slipped in and out of the Gators' key, signalling for the ball, but none of them could get open for more than a second.

. . . eight, seven, six . . .

Steve dove for the corner, but a much taller guard dogged him, blocking any pass.

. . . five, four, three . . .

The Cougar fans were on their feet, screaming. Jared knew the game was slipping away. He had no choice. He launched the ball from centre court.

Gators and Cougars alike stood frozen, all eyes following the ball from the tips of Jared's fingers. The buzzer sounded as the ball continued to climb. Reached the top of the arc. Curved downward toward the basket. And swished through the hoop. A perfect three-pointer.

The roar in the gymnasium was deafening.

Cougars 84, Gators 83.

* * *

"You'll certainly sleep tonight," Jared's mother said hoarsely as they walked from the bus stop toward their house. She reached over for what was probably the fifth time and hugged him close to her, this time even daring to plant a kiss on his forehead. Jared was so tired he didn't care. His mother was right. He *would* sleep tonight.

"I'm so proud of you, honey," she said again. "I thought I was going to burst!"

Jared smiled. He knew it wasn't much of one, but he was too tired to manufacture anything more convincing. It would have been great to feel like celebrating. His mom had offered to splurge and take them out to the Galaxy Grill for an all-you-can-eat supper, which was where Steve and his parents were now. It was Jared's favourite restaurant, and any other time he'd have given his left arm to go there.

But he wouldn't be able to keep a smile on his face all night. Sooner or later his mother would see through it, would want to know what was wrong.

No, he'd preferred to head home and grab a quick bite, take a shower, maybe watch Discovery Channel for a while, and then crawl into bed. He didn't want to spend the night talking about things he could no longer do anything about. What he really wanted to do was lie in the dark and play the movie of that last shot in his head nine or ten more times, if he could stay awake that long.

He could deal with the other stuff tomorrow. He was still a Cougar for a few more hours. Tonight was his. No one could take that away from him.

CHAPTER 19

"St. George!"

Jared, on his way to homeroom the next morning, turned to see Coach Jamieson standing in the school's atrium. The man didn't look happy. Jared sighed and walked toward him. "Hi, Coach," he said.

Mr. Jamieson didn't say anything, just beckoned for Jared to follow him to his office.

When Mr. Jamieson had closed the office door and turned to face him, Jared remembered a line the coach had used during practice: *Eyes tell us everything.* Jamieson's eyes were saying plenty. He knew about the math test.

"I had a visit from Mr. Keaton this morning," the coach said quietly.

Jared looked at his feet. "Yes, sir. I knew he'd be talking to you." His voice was little more than a whisper.

The coach folded his arms and leaned back against his desk, a wooden thing the size of a Buick and strewn with papers and schedules. "Jared," he said, "this came right out of the blue. Usually Mr. Keaton sees me ahead of time if one of my players is having trouble in his class."

Jared nodded. "I was havin' trouble a while ago, but then I got a handle on it."

The coach shook his head slowly. "You bombed the term test you wrote yesterday." He looked at Jared closely, his lips a thin line. "Is math the trouble you were referring to when we spoke during the game?"

Jared nodded.

"What happened?"

There was so much to tell, so much explaining to do, and Jared just didn't want to go there. "I guess I froze," he replied simply. "Forgot everything."

"Judging from the mark you made, I'd say that's exactly what happened. Maybe it's a test-anxiety problem." The coach ran a hand through his thinning brown hair. "Sometimes Mr. Keaton makes exceptions . . ." He trailed off, forcing a wry smile. "Well, actually, he's only made *one* exception. And that didn't work out so hot." Jared knew about the struggling student whom Mr. Keaton had let play on the team two years ago. The student was supposed to work extra hard to bring up his marks during the season, but it hadn't happened. Basketball had actually interfered with his work, taken time away from his studies. By January, the student was failing. He barely passed the year in June.

And Mr. Keaton had made no more exceptions.

"I didn't think he'd make one for me, either," Jared said. He reached into his backpack and pulled out his Cougar jersey. "Here, you'll be needin' this." Jared thought about Rafe wearing his number, and a hard knot formed in his chest.

The coach held up his hands. "No, I don't want you to turn it in yet."

Jared looked at him, surprised.

"You were doing fine in math for a while. Mr. Keaton said so, too. Maybe you know that material better than you think." Jared's unspoken question must have been evident on his face because the coach continued, "Maybe Mr. Keaton will let you do a rewrite."

Hope welled up inside Jared for a moment, then just as quickly vanished. He remembered the policy Mr. Keaton had told them the first day of school, the one printed in bold lettering on the notice he'd sent home to parents. "Mr. Keaton don't allow test rewrites," Jared told the coach. "He lets us redo quizzes as many times as we want, but not tests." He stretched out his hand, still holding the jersey.

Coach Jamieson shook his head. "Maybe in this case he would. I think it's worth a shot to ask him, anyway. Trust me, it'd be a lot easier for me just to give that jersey to someone else—"

Jared was grateful the coach hadn't said Rafe's name.

"—but I think you're worth the extra mile, Jared. You played one heck of a game yesterday. And I'm not just talking about that last shot." His eyes twinkled as he spoke, "Although that was one beautiful basket." He put his hand on Jared's shoulder. "Once you got into the game, you played better than some guys in high school. And it's not just mechanics, all the form and function stuff. Anyone can learn that. What they can't learn are the instincts I've seen in you these past few weeks. Basketball's in your blood. I'd like to keep it there."

Coach Jamieson opened the door of his office. "It's worth a try, isn't it? Go talk to Mr. Keaton about a rewrite. What's the worst that can happen? He says no. So what? You're no further behind than you are now."

"I'll ask him," Jared said, returning the jersey to his backpack. "Thanks, Coach. For everything."

Heading toward homeroom, Jared heard Coach Jamieson's question echo again and again in his head. *What's the worst that can happen?* There were a lot worse things than hearing the answer "no." He knew that. One of them was seeing the face of someone you had betrayed.

CHAPTER 20

Jared had hoped to talk to Mr. Keaton before homeroom, but the teacher wasn't at his desk when Jared got there. Pete said the secretary had called him over the PA for a phone call, and the teacher had left, all red in the face. But smiling.

By the time the teacher returned—the smile still plainly evident—the few remaining moments were taken up with attendance, announcements, and the collection of chocolate bar sales money from the school's latest fundraising campaign. Jared made a mental note to bring in the money for the six bars he'd taken home. He hadn't actually sold them. They'd been lying on his desk in his bedroom since last weekend, and each of them had begun calling his name in smooth, chocolatey voices.

He'd have to ask his mom for an advance on his allowance. She wouldn't be impressed when she heard what use it had been put to, especially since she hadn't gotten to enjoy any of the bars herself.

Jared had forgotten what day of the schedule it was—he now scanned the large calendar at the front of the room and saw it was Day 3—and he grimaced when he realized math was first period. He spent most of the class hoping they wouldn't be getting their tests back. Although he knew Mr. Keaton had marked his, he hoped the teacher hadn't had time to mark them all, since he'd been at the game the night before.

No such luck.

"I want to congratulate a few people for their outstanding performance on the math test yesterday," he said just before the period ended. He opened a thick folder and pulled out three tests. He handed the first one to Ellie. "You made a perfect mark, Ellie. Not a single mistake. Well done, indeed." As usual, no one else in the room said anything, and Jared saw Rafe and a couple others make some rude gestures that Mr. Keaton didn't see. "You made second highest, Rafe." Pete and Kyle and a couple of others whistled as Rafe walked to the front of the room to get his test. "And third highest," continued the teacher, "goes to Sasha."

Sasha Rivers squealed her surprise, which brought a burst of laughter from the rest of the class. She almost ran up the aisle to get her test. "My dad's gonna faint when he sees this," she trilled. "Maybe I'll get my cellphone back now."

"Glad to bring peace to one household," said Mr. Keaton. Then his face took on a solemn expression. "There were some other strong marks, too, and there were also a few that weren't so strong. I'd like all of you to get these signed this evening." He hefted the folder in preparation for passing back the remaining test papers. "I've written a note on a few of them for students to see me. I'll be available at recess and lunchtime if anyone would like to talk then."

Jared didn't need to raise his eyes to know the teacher was looking directly at him.

* * *

"So how'd you do, Jared?" Rafe asked at recess. He and Pete and Kyle had come up to Jared on the outdoor courts, interrupting the three on three that he and Steve were involved in. Rafe's blue Hilfiger shirt and tan pants seemed adult amid the sweats and hoodies the other boys were wearing. But the expression on his face made him appear far younger than eleven years. He looked like a little kid who'd just gotten everything he wanted for his birthday. Including the pony.

Real subtle, thought Jared. Not like his father, apparently. Jared had heard the principal, Mr. Rideout, joking about him to Mr. Keaton in the hallway the day the school board announced Skylar Wells's donation of computers to the school. Mr. Rideout was saying that, when they were in university together, Skylar Wells could start a conversation with you about the weather and end up knowing your bank balance and shoe size. Even then, Jared didn't think he'd care to spend much time with a person like that.

"Yo! Jared!" Rafe snapped. "The math test. What'd you make?"

The test. As far as Jared had heard, only one other person had made a lower mark than he did—Su Mei Hyun, the Korean student who had arrived from Seoul a week earlier and spoke very little English. Give her a couple more months with the language, though, and Jared was sure even Su Mei would rank near the top of the class. He shrugged. "I flunked it," he said.

Pete smiled sympathetically. "Join the club, buddy."

"Pete made thirty-nine percent," Rafe said. "Do any worse than that?"

"You takin' a survey?" Steve asked dryly when he ambled over to see what had interrupted the action.

Rafe ignored him. He looked at Jared. "Well?"

Jared sighed. "I made twenty-one," he said, avoiding Steve's eyes. "I think I got part of that for spelling my name right."

Rafe whistled. "Too bad," he offered, but the smile on his face contradicted the sincerity of his words.

The three sauntered off, leaving Jared to face Steve, his mouth hanging open in disbelief. *"You made twenty-one?"* Steve demanded. "You didn't even tell me you'd got it *back!*"

"Forget it, okay?" Jared growled. He wanted just ten minutes without thinking about math or anything else. Ten minutes to forget everything but how good it felt to drive a basketball to the hoop. "Just drop it."

Steve let the basketball fall to his feet, and it bounced and rolled off to one side.

"You guys playin' or what?" shouted Kenny, the third guy on their team.

Steve waved him off. "You got yourself a three on two," he said and walked off the court.

Jared caught up with him. "Look, I was gonna tell you—"

"When?" asked Steve, still walking. "Christmas?"

"Look, Steve, some weird stuff's been happenin' lately—"

Steve stopped and looked at his friend sharply. "Jeez, Jared, you ain't doin' drugs, are you?"

Jared shook his head. "No, nothin' like that. C'mere." He moved over to one of the benches by the court and sat down. Steve sat beside him, and Jared began to explain the events of the last few days.

"But tellin' Rafe you were *cheatin'!*" exclaimed Steve when Jared had finished. "What were you *thinkin'*, man?"

Jared shrugged. "I *wasn't* thinkin'," he said.

"And Ellie," Steve said. "Think how that musta made *her* feel."

"Since when did Ellie Brejovic become *your* best friend?"

Steve scowled. "Look, I don't even *know* her. But there's one thing I *do* know. I wouldn't do to my worst enemy what you did to Ellie. Especially after everything she did to help you."

Jared leaned forward with his arms on his knees, looking down at a crack in the pavement. A solitary ant struggled to drag a leaf many times its size across the crack and, although the task looked impossible, it was not giving up. Jared reached down and lifted the ant and its burden across the crack, but the ant dropped the leaf and ran for cover. It seemed like there just wasn't anything Jared couldn't screw up. He sighed. "You're right. I was an idiot."

"So now you're gonna ask about a rewrite?" Steve asked.

"Jamieson thinks it's worth a shot."

"And what d'*you* think?"

Jared looked out to the soccer field beyond the basketball courts, watching as a gust of wind shook the branches of the maple trees growing along the edge of the school's property. A curtain of leaves tore loose and corkscrewed earthward, the motion like liquid spiralling down a drain. Like water flushed down a toilet.

Which kind of summed up what he thought of his chances.

* * *

Jared had waited until near the end of the lunch break to talk to Mr. Keaton, thinking that no one else would be around. But he'd been waiting in the hallway for nearly ten minutes, and Mr. Keaton was still talking to the student ahead of him. Finally, the classroom door opened and Pete came out. He sighed wearily when he saw Jared. "He says I'm gonna have to pull out all the stops for the next unit."

Jared knocked on the door. "Mr. Keaton?"

"Come in."

Jared entered, leaving the door ajar behind him. He was fairly sure this wouldn't be a long meeting.

The teacher looked up from a note he was writing in his record book, then put his pen down. "Jared. I'm glad you're here." He leaned back in his chair. "What happened?" he asked simply.

Jared sat down in the chair across from the teacher. He lifted his shoulders and let them drop. His answer was as simple as the teacher's question: "I forgot it all."

Mr. Keaton shook his head. "That would appear to be true," he said. "Ordinarily, I'd go over the test with you, point out places where you'd gone wrong, but you went wrong almost everywhere."

Jared nodded. "I know."

"Did you try the review I gave you?"

"Yeah. I spent a couple hours on it."

"Did you work on it with Ellie?"

Jared shook his head.

The teacher raised his eyebrows and seemed about to ask a question but did not. "You realize what this means."

Jared swallowed, glancing at the door to make sure no one else was waiting to see Mr. Keaton. He had thought he'd heard something, a footstep maybe, but he couldn't see anyone. "Mr. Keaton . . ." he began.

"Yes, Jared?"

"I was wonderin' if, you know, if maybe it might be possible for me to . . ."

"To what, Jared?"

"To rewrite the test." There. He'd said it.

The teacher sat forward in his chair, picked up his pen and rolled it between his hands a couple of times. Jared could see he was taking his time before answering, making sure he knew exactly what he wanted to say before he said it. "Jared, you know I have a policy about not allowing rewrites."

"Yes, sir."

Keaton leaned back in his chair. "Do you know why I have that policy?" he asked.

Jared looked down at his hands. They were calloused from all the ball-handling, and for a moment he wondered if his brain looked like that from banging against math. He looked up. "I guess so no one has an advantage over anyone else?"

The teacher shook his head. "Not really. If I were ever to give a rewrite, I'd make up a whole new test."

"Then why?" Jared asked.

"It's about commitment," said Mr. Keaton. "You know I let my students rewrite quizzes as many times as they want."

"Yes, sir."

"I do that because I think students need the opportunity to learn from their mistakes. Sometimes they may do poorly simply because they weren't prepared to be quizzed on a concept in that particular way, not because they don't know the work." He put his pen down. "But the term test is that point where the rubber meets the road. Do you know what I mean by that?"

"I think so. You want to see exactly what we can do. Like when Coach Jamieson really makes us pour it on at the end of practice."

The teacher nodded. "Something like that, yes. And I

go to great lengths to prepare my students for term tests. At least I think I do. I *hope* I do."

Jared thought back to how the teacher had described what the test would look like, had made up a review to help them practice, had even divided the class into groups to attempt sample questions in the days before the test. He looked at his hands again. "You do."

"That test shouldn't be a surprise to anyone when he or she finally sees it." The teacher sighed. "But for some reason, it was a surprise to you. Right?"

Jared flushed. "It wasn't really . . ." he began. "I just . . . It's just that . . ." He looked at the teacher. "I guess I wasn't as ready as I thought I was."

The teacher smiled. It was a friendly smile, though, a sympathetic smile. Jared knew Mr. Keaton wasn't making fun of his comment or situation. "The rubber met the road, Jared. And the road turned out to be a lot rougher than you were prepared for. But, fortunately, we've got the remainder of the year to address your weaknesses." He seemed to underline the phrase *the remainder of the year* with his voice.

Jared didn't say anything. There was nothing to say.

"You played an incredible game yesterday, Jared. I knew you were good, but I had no idea just how strong you are on the court."

Jared waited.

"Although you're going to miss this season, I'm sure you'll be Mr. Jamieson's first choice for next year's lineup."

Jared got up to leave. He was tired of talking. Tired of listening. Tired of everything.

"I know you'll find this hard to believe, but this is for your own good."

"Right." He made his way toward the door.

"Remember, I'll be happy to give you as much extra help as you need."

"Uh-huh." As Jared reached the door, he saw the flash of someone disappearing around the corner.

Someone had been listening.

Someone wearing a blue shirt.

CHAPTER 21

Jared threw the worn tennis ball as hard as he could, then watched as the yellow Lab streaked across the grass, catching the ball in mid-air on the first bounce and strutting jauntily back to drop it at Jared's feet. No matter how many times he threw it, Cal always awaited the next toss with trembling anticipation. The dog's bright eyes tracked the ball in Jared's hand like lasers, and his body coiled with excitement each time Jared brought his arm back for the throw.

Sometimes, Jared would only pretend to throw the ball, elaborately bringing his arm back and then shooting it forward, pantomiming its release. At those times, Cal would race across the park in the direction of the toss, scanning the sky for his prize, then abruptly stop, his head low, tail drooping. It was as if he were embarrassed at having made such a spectacle of himself, and he'd return to Jared by a roundabout route, as though to give the impression that he'd only gone for a stroll. All the while, he'd give Jared a reproving stare as if not quite believing Jared would stoop so low as to fool him. But all Jared had to do was raise the ball again, and the spell would be broken. Cal, ball-chaser extraordinaire, was back.

"Last time, buddy," Jared said, although if he had his way, he'd have stayed and thrown till midnight. But he had to go home sometime. He threw the ball once more and, as he waited for the dog to return with it, he thought of the math test in his backpack that he needed to have his mother sign. This was going to be, without question, a much bigger deal than showing her Mr. Keaton's note last month about his work sliding. Hopefully, though, she'd recognize that he'd been trying. Jeez, he'd spent as many as four sessions a week with Ellie, and the results had been pretty amazing. For *him,* anyway. Heck, for *anybody!*

His thoughts turned to Ellie, and he wondered what she was doing at that moment. Feeding her fish? Iguana-proofing her apartment for her lizard-phobic housekeeper? He grinned at that last thought. *Jacques*. What better name to give an exotic creature than that of the person who had explored faraway oceans?

And what better person than Ellie to help Jared find his way through the math that had mystified him for so long? *Think how that musta made* her *feel*. Jared felt another wave of regret pass over him as he remembered what Steve had said that day at recess. *I wouldn't do to my worst enemy what you did to Ellie. Especially after everything she did to help you.*

Steve was right. What a jerk he'd been. Pretending to be *cheating* rather than let anyone know he'd been spending time with Ellie. What kind of loser was *that*?

Cal whined and Jared realized the dog had returned and dropped the ball at his feet and was waiting for another throw. "Sorry, buddy, no can do. Time's up." Jared picked up the ball and returned it to the can with the others.

The dog lowered his head, his tail drooping toward the ground.

"Cal," Jared muttered, rubbing the dog's ears, "believe me, there's nothing you can do that'll make me feel worse than I already do." He sighed long and loudly. "I guess I just have a talent for lettin' people down. You, too, huh?"

He clipped the leash onto the dog's collar and headed home.

* * *

Walking up the driveway, Jared could hear the radio on in the kitchen and knew his mother was making supper.

Should he wait until after they'd eaten, or should he just get it over with now? Like it mattered.

It was, however, a decision he didn't have to make.

"Jared, honey," his mother said as he came in the door. Several expressions flickered across her face one after the other and so quickly that Jared couldn't tell if she was angry or upset. "Sit down, dear."

Now he knew. He was in trouble. He sat down.

"Mr. Keaton called me this afternoon," she said. "At work."

Jared scowled. "Jeez, does that guy have nothin' better to do than get on my case? I was *gonna* tell you myself. *Really*."

Another expression settled over her face, this time one of surprise. "But he said you didn't know."

"For Pete's sake, I got it back first thing this mornin'. And I already knew I'd failed anyway. Jeez, I left *out* most of the freakin' questions!" Jared slumped in his chair, annoyed with the world. It seemed like this math test was going to haunt him for the rest of his life.

"Sweetheart, I know about the test. That's not what I'm talking about."

He looked up. "Then what?"

"Mr. Keaton is going to let you rewrite it. Tomorrow after school. If you do well on that one, he won't count the one you wrote yesterday. And you'll still be able to play for the Cougars."

It took a long moment for his mother's news to sink in. After all that talk about why he never gave rewrites, here was Keaton offering him a second chance. Jared shook his head. Clearly, he'd stepped into that bizarre parallel universe again, the one where all the faces were the same but the people wearing them were suddenly different, no longer who they seemed to be.

But so what? Jared sat up straight. As weird as Keaton's change of heart was, Jared wasn't about to blow it. He was determined to make the most of what was certainly a once-only opportunity. He'd sit down again and go through his math from beginning to end, thinking about all the things Ellie had told him. He'd think about bingo chips and Kraft Dinner boxes and all the other real-world examples she'd talked about. He'd think about drawing diagrams and looking for patterns. He would read questions five or six times if he had to, really try to focus on what information was necessary and what was not.

He could *do* this. After all, Ellie had shown him how, hadn't she? He wasn't going to let himself down again. And he wasn't letting *her* down, either. Not if he could help it.

CHAPTER 22

"Time's up," Mr. Keaton said.

Jared pushed his chair back from the table. "That's okay. I was done, anyway. I was just checkin' over my work."

The teacher whistled. "Jared St. George checking over his work. I'm alerting the media."

Jared smiled as he picked up his test and the package of math manipulatives and carried them to the teacher's desk. "I wanna thank you again for lettin' me rewrite this. Even if I don't do so hot, I know it was a lot to ask you to make up a new test and then stay after school on a Friday afternoon so I could write it. Especially since you don't usually do this."

The teacher stood up and came around from behind

his desk. "Let's just say I listened to some pretty convincing arguments to the contrary."

In the middle of stapling his papers together, Jared looked up. "Coach Jamieson talked to you, didn't he?"

The teacher grimaced, then smiled noncommittally. "I, ah . . . that person made me promise not to tell."

Jared shook his head in wonder. Coach Jamieson. He'd heard before how loyal he was to his players, but even this seemed like a lot to do for a first-year Cougar. Jamieson was quite a guy. Jared wondered how he might thank him without letting him know Mr. Keaton had tipped him off.

The teacher took the test but didn't put it into his briefcase. Instead, he slowly flipped through it.

"I tried every question this time," Jared said.

"I see you did. I'm impressed."

"I know I probably made tons 'a mistakes, but at least I *felt* like I knew what I was doin' this time."

"Well, it's not because this test was easier than the last one. If anything, I made it a little tougher."

Jared grinned. "Gee, thanks."

"You're welcome," the teacher smiled in return. "It was the least I could do."

Jared slipped his backpack over his shoulder and headed toward the door. "Mr. Keaton?" Jared turned toward the teacher.

"Yes, Jared?"

"Will you, you know, be able to mark it over the weekend?"

The teacher shook his head. "'Fraid not. I have family things that'll keep me pretty busy tomorrow and Sunday."

Jared's face fell. "Oh." He turned to leave.

"So I planned to mark it right now."

Jared looked back to see the teacher's deadpan face crease into another smile. Mr. Keaton glanced at his watch. "How about I give you a call later this evening and let you know how you did?"

"Jeez, that'd be *great!*" He was about to leave when he stopped and turned. "You know, if you're real busy you don't have to—"

"I *want* to. Now get out of here, okay?"

* * *

Jared had walked Cal, played some one on one with Steve in the driveway, eaten supper, done the dishes, finished all his homework, and watched nearly an hour of TV—which included at least three Skylar Wells for Mayor campaign commercials—and Mr. Keaton *still* hadn't phoned. He looked at his watch. Three minutes to nine. He surfed the channels, looking for something decent to watch, but found nothing—even the Discovery Channel offered nothing that he wanted to see. Another installment of that reality show with the ex-partners was just about to start, but he certainly wasn't going to waste his time on *that*. He looked at his watch again. One minute to nine.

His mother came up from the basement with a load of laundry, waiting since Monday to be folded, under her arm. Friday night in the St. George household—the excitement never stopped. "He hasn't called yet?" she asked.

"Uh-uh."

"Maybe he got tied up with something at school. Or maybe he's at his sister's again."

Jared turned to her. "At his sister's? I didn't even know he *had* a sister. Why would he be there?"

His mother set the laundry basket on the sofa, sat down, and began to sort and fold the clothes, glancing at the television screen as Jared flipped through the channels again. "She broke her ankle skateboarding," she said as she separated towels from face cloths.

"Mr. Keaton has a sister who *skateboards?*"

His mom looked over at him. "I . . . I guess I heard that somewhere. Apparently, she's very good. Provincial champion two years running."

Jared shook his head. "I didn't think old people skateboarded."

"She's younger than he is. She's still in university." His

mother paused. "And he's not *that* old, you know. He's *my* age."

Tired of surfing, Jared muted the television. The opening credits for the reality program had begun to roll. Turning to his mother, he asked, "How do you know all this, anyway?"

She looked at him, looked at the clothing she was folding, and then at him again. "Jared, there's something I've been meaning to—"

The phone rang. "I bet that's him now," she said, reaching for the cordless. "Hello?" Her eyes lit up. "Hi, we were waiting for your call. Jared's been dying to know what he—" She paused. Her eyes widened. "*Really?* Well, that's fan—"

Jared's mother stopped talking. She laid down the towel she was holding and listened to the voice on the other end of the line for what seemed a long time. There were moments when she would start to ask a question or make a comment, but then she'd stop and continue to listen, nodding her head. Finally, she said, "Okay, I'll tell him. We'll be there."

She listened as the caller said something again. "I know," she replied. "*No* one has." Pause. "Right. Talk to you soon. Bye." Jared's mother clicked the phone off and set it down. She didn't take her hand off it, though. It was as if she'd been caught in a snapshot, a moment frozen in time.

"Mom?" Jared switched off the television. "What's wrong?"

His mother didn't appear to hear him. She sat looking at the darkened television screen as though watching a program only she could see.

"Mom?" Jared got up and moved to the sofa, sitting beside her. "You're scaring me." He said it as a joke, but the words held some truth.

His mother picked up the towel on her lap and folded it neatly. "Well, slugger," she said, "looks like you aced your math test."

"Really? You're kiddin'. What'd I make?"

"Eighty-eight percent."

"No way! *Really?*"

His mother nodded. "Really."

Jared leaped from the sofa and capered about the room. "Eighty-eight percent!" He strutted back and forth in front of his mother, his arms raised in victory, his whoops loud enough to shake the windows. Cal began to bark at this unusual display, and Jared took the dog's front paws and led the barking animal in a noisy, halting dance across the living room.

His mother finally managed to make herself heard above the racket. "Jared!"

He turned to her. "Yeah?"

"There's a problem."

"Whaddya mean 'a problem'?"

"Honey, I think you'd better sit down."

CHAPTER 23

The wide hallway was filled with people. Jared was surprised to see so many men and women at the school board office on a Saturday. Didn't people get weekends off anymore? Then he realized that only a few of them wore the nametags that identified them as board personnel. Several of them seemed to be members of the public, like his mother and himself. Then he saw the videocameras and the microphones.

A young woman wearing a grey jacket and skirt approached Jared and his mom, who were sitting on chairs beside a closed door bearing a sign that read BOARDROOM. The door was a dark, richly-carved wood, and the handle was a fancy, brass affair that seemed altogether far more knob than any door really needed, especially one that didn't even lead outside. Jared wondered why anyone would spend that much money on a door and then buy chairs as uncomfortable as the wooden ones he and his mother were sitting on. Very modern, with lots of lines and angles, but he had to keep moving his butt around to keep it from going numb. Of course, maybe that was the point. Maybe you weren't *supposed* to sit on them. Maybe they were designed to keep people from hanging around too long. Well, that was okay by him. He'd leave right now if he could. If it hadn't been for that jerk Rafe, he wouldn't be here in the first place.

The woman stopped in front of them. "Ms. St. George?"

Jared's mother looked up, and Jared felt her draw back instinctively. "Yes?" she replied, but her voice sounded tight, much different from the voice Jared was used to.

"Then you must be Jared," the woman said, turning toward him.

Jared nodded.

"I'm Diana Barnes with Channel 6 News. I was wondering if I could ask the two of you—"

"Excuse me," his mother interrupted, "but we really don't wish to speak to reporters. This isn't a media event. It's a personal matter."

The woman looked at her in the same way Jared had seen adults look at him in the past. As though his mother was a kid and this Barnes woman was the adult who knew what was best. "It's a little naive of you to think that, isn't it?" She turned and indicated the growing number of people milling about. Two men who had just arrived were setting up a tripod with lights opposite the closed door.

"I'm not sure how this got so blown out of proportion," Jared's mother said, "but it's still a personal matter."

"Anything that involves a candidate for mayor, especially someone as well known as Skylar Wells, is news, Ms. St. George. May I call you Terri?"

"No, you may not," and Jared heard in those four words the spirit he was used to hearing in his mother's voice. "And I really have nothing to say to you. I'd appreciate it if you'd leave us alone."

The newswoman's eyes widened. She sniffed, then drew herself up to her full height. In her high heels, she was an imposing figure, close to six feet, and for a moment Jared couldn't help but think she'd make a terrific basketball player. When the woman spoke again, her voice was icy. "You'll be on camera whether you want to be or not, Ms. St. George. I'm just offering you an opportunity to tell your side."

"I believe," Jared's mother said evenly, "that's what the *meeting* is for."

The newswoman shook her head as if finding it difficult to believe anyone would say no to being on camera. She looked at her watch, then nodded her head toward the end of the hallway. The elevator doors were just opening. "Don't say I didn't warn you. You're about to see how it's *really* done." She moved off down the hallway, a camera operator and a lighting technician in tow.

From the elevator stepped Rafe and his father, Alderman Skylar Wells. Both wore navy blue suits, Rafe's a smaller version of the alderman's but both looking like they cost an arm and a leg. The alderman's perfect white teeth seemed almost luminous as he flashed them at the cameras pointed in his direction. He paused in his step, allowing the newspeople the opportunity to gather around and ask their questions.

"Alderman Wells, can you tell us the purpose of today's meeting of the school board?" asked a man in a brown jacket.

"Certainly, Dave. Superintendent Carolyn Janes has convened a special meeting of the board's executive to address an act of blatant unprofessionalism on the part of a teacher at Cornwallis Middle School."

"And are you the person who laid the complaint?" the man asked.

"I most certainly am," the alderman replied. "It was my son, Rafe, here, who brought the actions of this teacher to my attention." He put his hands on Rafe's shoulders.

"Rafe," said another newsperson. "How does it feel to be the centre of so much controversy?"

Even from this distance, Jared could see Rafe struggle to keep from smiling. "It's not something I like," he said, "but when a teacher does something wrong, a person needs to stand up for what's right. Even if it means that people may not like you much for doing it."

Jared wondered how many times Rafe had practised those two sentences. He pictured Rafe standing in front of a full-length mirror all morning wearing that same suit and saying those same stupid sentences over and over. Jared wanted to kick his butt.

His mother seemed to read his thoughts. She placed her hand on his arm and squeezed gently.

"Alderman Wells," said Diana Barnes, "can you tell us more about the alleged unprofessionalism that resulted in today's special meeting of the school board?"

Wells shook his head, a sad expression on his face. "Diana, I wish I could go into more detail, but let me just say this. When a teacher makes decisions about students based on personal reasons rather than on sound educational practice, that teacher has no place in the classroom. As my son just said, speaking out for what is right is often not the popular course to follow. But I am committed to doing the right thing, as I have always been. My entire career in the private sector and my years as an alderman have been based on that very principle. What better lesson can we teach our youth today than to speak out against injustice, to speak out against unfairness, to speak out against the kinds of actions that give special consideration to some while ignoring the valuable contributions of others? I say there is *no* better lesson than that."

Wells nodded and smiled as cameras flashed and recorders rolled, then he guided Rafe down the hallway toward the boardroom door. Rafe shot Jared a look that showed just how much he was enjoying himself, and Jared felt his mother's hand squeeze his arm again, this time more tightly. At that moment, the door opened and a man ushered the alderman and his son inside.

Diana Barnes stopped at the door along with the other media people, who were not permitted to enter the boardroom. *"That,"* she said to Jared's mother with a mixture of awe and disdain in her voice, "is how it's done."

* * *

Jared and his mother didn't need to be in the boardroom to know what Rafe and Skylar Wells were telling the members of the school board. Mr. Keaton had told Jared's mom most of it on the phone the night before. Rafe, he explained, had found out that the teacher had allowed Jared to rewrite the test, and Rafe was telling everyone that it was because Mr. Keaton was dating Jared's mother. He'd seen them walking together in the park one day. Only briefly, but long enough to realize he wasn't witnessing a parent-teacher interview.

Jared had been dumbfounded by the news. Mr. Keaton and his *mother*? *Dating*? Apparently, that bizarre parallel universe was working overtime.

But the news about his mother's new boyfriend hadn't been nearly as unsettling as its implication. "So *you* convinced him to let me rewrite the test," he said to her the night before. He looked down at the living room carpet, stained and worn in so many places. His mother had often commented about wanting to replace it, but there was never enough money. "If you don't look too closely," she'd said after going over their household budget yet again, "it doesn't seem so bad." But Jared *was* looking closely, and it looked crummy. Which exactly described the way he felt. He probably hadn't made eighty-eight percent on the test after all. All of this was just one big joke. On *him*.

His mother reached across the sofa to him, tried to put her hand on his shoulder, but he shrugged her off, got up and walked to the window and stood there looking out at the night. "Jared," she said from the sofa, "despite what you're thinking, I didn't ask Ron to let you rewrite it. I'd never do that."

Ron! He'd never have imagined her using his teacher's first name, either. It sounded weird. Before this year, he'd never even thought of teachers *having* first names. And now his mother was dating one. *His.*

"Honey," she continued, "I didn't even know you'd

failed it until he called with the news, and by then he'd already decided to give you the second test."

But this didn't make Jared feel any better. "So what? He was doing it for you, anyway."

His mother came up behind him and put her hands on his shoulders, turning him around to face her. "Do you really think that's the kind of man Ron is? That that's the kind of thing he would do?"

Jared looked down at the carpet again. "I dunno," he said.

"I think you do." She gave him a nudge. "And even if you didn't, do you think I'd want to go out with a man who *would* do something like that?"

Jared shrugged again.

"Are you *forgetting* DVD Guy?" she asked.

As miserable as Jared was feeling at that moment, he had to smile at her. "No," he admitted, "I guess you *wouldn't* want to go out with a guy like that."

"Well, I'm glad we agree on *that* much," she said. Pushing aside her carefully folded laundry, his mother sat back down on the sofa and patted the cushion beside her. When Jared sat down too, she took both his hands and looked him straight in the eyes. "You know, it was for this very reason that I didn't tell you I was seeing him. He *wanted* me to tell you, but I didn't want you or anyone else to think you were getting special treatment." She squeezed his hands. "Ron let you rewrite the test because someone went to see him and convinced him it was the right thing to do. End of story."

"Who, then?" Jared asked.

"He wouldn't say. He told me he'd given his word that he wouldn't tell."

"Coach Jamieson?"

"Maybe. Probably. I don't think it matters. What *does* matter is that Ron decided you deserved another chance to show him what you'd learned. And you did." She smiled wryly. "You know, Jared, he said on the phone that he marked the rewrite much harder than the first test. And I believe him."

Jared's face mirrored his surprise. "He told *me* it was a harder test."

"See? He didn't take it easy on you. And I wouldn't have *wanted* him to."

Jared nodded. "So what's all the fuss about?"

His mother let go of his hands and sighed. "Just before Ron left his classroom this afternoon, the principal came to see him about a phone call he'd gotten from the superintendent of schools. The superintendent told him she'd received a complaint about unfair treatment. There's going to be a special meeting of the school board tomorrow afternoon to look into it."

"Tomorrow? That's Saturday. Who meets on a Saturday?"

His mother reached for the folded clothes and began

piling them neatly in the hamper. "Ron said it almost never happens. The one time he's heard about was an emergency." She paused for a moment before continuing, "Apparently, someone with a lot of pull made it happen."

Jared whistled. "Jeez, is Mr. Keaton in trouble?"

"Well, he didn't do anything wrong."

"That's not what I asked."

His mother looked at him and smiled, but it was a hollow, fleeting expression.

This time it was Jared who squeezed *her* hands. "It's gonna be okay, Mom," he said.

* * *

Now, though, Jared wasn't so sure. Mr. Keaton had called that morning with an update, saying he'd learned it was Rafe's father who had lodged the complaint. He'd heard it on the news, a twenty-second blurb about Alderman Wells waging a personal campaign for integrity in education. Ordinarily, information about disputes like this didn't make it into the media, but Skylar Wells had decided to go public because he felt his family's privacy wasn't as important as the ethical issue involved. The name of the teacher in question wouldn't be released—but all the students in 6K would know immediately that the story was about Mr. Keaton.

"So all this is just about Rafe not getting to play for the Cougars, isn't it?" Jared had asked his mother that morning.

"I think that's certainly part of it," she had replied.

And now Jared understood clearly what the other part was. It was about Skylar Wells getting to stand in front of TV cameras. He'd already done it when he donated the computers to the school, and now he was doing it again. Not only was he generous beyond belief, he was concerned for the educational well-being of every child in the city. What better person could there be for mayor than Skylar Wells?

Jared wanted to throw up.

Just then the boardroom door opened and a man beckoned for them to enter.

CHAPTER 24

"Jared, do you know why we've requested that you and your mother come here today?" asked the woman sitting opposite him. She had introduced herself as Carolyn Janes, Superintendent of Schools, and the men on her left and right as Assistant Superintendent Richard Wilcox, and Director of Human Resources Chandra Malavi. Jared thought about how many decisions these three people made every day that directly affected him and students like him, yet this was the first time he had laid eyes on any of them.

At the far end of the table sat Mr. Keaton and a woman who was introduced as his teachers' union representative, Sandra Conrad. Mr. Keaton had already given his statement, and he was allowed to listen to the statements of the various parties involved, but he was not permitted to ask questions or to comment. It was clearly the three people sitting across from Jared who were in charge of the proceedings.

Jared looked at his mother, who sat beside him at the table, and he nodded his head. It was the longest, widest table he'd ever seen. You could put every kid in 6K around that table and still have room for some of the Cougars. "You want me to tell you about the math test I rewrote," he replied. He wondered what Rafe had told these people. Rafe and his father had left before Jared and his mother had entered the room.

"Actually," the woman said, "we'd like you to tell us *how* you came to write it."

Jared looked again at his mother, who smiled her support, then proceeded to tell them about how poorly he'd done on the first test and how his basketball coach, Mr. Jamieson, had encouraged him to ask for a rewrite.

"Did you think that was a fair request?" asked Mr. Malavi, who was writing notes on a thick pad of paper.

"I told him I didn't think Mr. Keaton would let me do it because he said at the beginning of the year he only lets students rewrite quizzes, not tests."

"But Mr. Jamieson coaxed you to ask Mr. Keaton anyway," said Mr. Malavi.

Jared frowned. "I don't know about *coaxed*. He said it

was worth a shot. The worst that could happen was Mr. Keaton would say no." Jared smiled over at the teacher, and the teacher smiled in return.

"But, instead, he said yes," clarified Ms. Janes.

Jared was surprised by her statement. "No, he didn't. He said no."

Ms. Janes looked confused, and glanced down at the pad of paper in front of her. It undoubtedly contained notes from her conversation with Rafe and his father. "Excuse me?" she asked. "He said no?"

Jared nodded.

It was Mr. Wilcox, the assistant superintendent, who spoke next. "But then Mr. Keaton changed his mind and said yes."

"Yeah, I guess so," said Jared.

Mr. Wilcox scowled at him, and Jared got the feeling that Mr. Wilcox was annoyed that Jared was taking so much of his valuable time. "So, just to be clear, before you left Mr. Keaton's office, you made arrangements to rewrite the test."

Jared shook his head. "No. Did Rafe tell you that?"

Mr. Malavi spoke up. "There seems to be a discrepancy between what Rafe had to say and what Mr. Keaton has told us. We're hoping you can clear this up."

Now Jared was getting annoyed. Rafe had been listening outside Mr. Keaton's classroom that afternoon, so he *knew* the teacher had said no. Had Rafe lied to them?

"What happened was, I asked Mr. Keaton if I could rewrite the test and he told me no."

"And that's all?" Ms. Janes asked.

"Well, we talked a bit about why he felt he couldn't let me do it, but yeah, that's pretty much it."

"I'm confused," said Mr. Malavi. "You *did* rewrite the test, didn't you?"

Jared nodded. "Mr. Keaton called later that day and said he'd changed his mind."

"Did he tell you why?" asked Ms. Janes.

"He said the next day that he'd listened to some pretty good arguments about why he should let me rewrite it."

"And who made those arguments?"

Jared shrugged. "I don't know."

Ms. Janes looked at Jared's mother. "Ms. St. George, are *you* the person who persuaded Mr. Keaton to change his mind?"

Jared could feel his mother grow tense. "No," she replied, "I am not."

Mr. Wilcox frowned. "You can see, can't you, how we might find that difficult to believe, given your personal relationship with Mr. Keaton?"

Jared heard a sudden intake of breath beside him. "And you can see, can't you," she replied, "how I might find that question offensive?" Jared could hear anger flare beneath her words. *Good for you, Mom,* he thought.

Ms. Janes quickly spoke up, her tone softer than Mr.

Wilcox's, but her manner much the same. "It's not our intention to offend anyone, Ms. St. George, but someone spoke to Mr. Keaton and said something that changed a policy he has adhered to for several years and even put into writing for parents. Doesn't it seem reasonable that you might have been that person, given that you and Mr. Keaton now see each other socially and Jared needed to make a good mark on that test to continue playing basketball?"

His mother's face was as red as Jared had ever seen it, including the morning when DVD Guy suggested she was the sort of person who'd welcome having stolen electronics in her home. He saw her grip the edge of the table, and for a moment he thought she might actually get up from her chair and let loose. But she didn't. "I'd like to ask a question, if I may."

"By all means," said Ms. Janes.

"Isn't a teacher's policies in the classroom his own business? I find it hard to believe so much uproar has been caused by something as insignificant as allowing a student to rewrite a test."

Ms. Janes nodded. "Mr. Keaton is well within his rights as a teacher to assess his students as he sees fit. It isn't his decision to allow Jared to rewrite the test that we're calling into question. We're questioning *why* he did so. If there has been some impropriety here, we need to address it."

Mr. Wilcox had more to add on the subject. "Teachers shape their students in many ways, not only educating them through the lessons they teach but also acting as role models in the way they live their lives in relation to their students. Actions often speak louder than words, and if Mr. Keaton has acted inappropriately, there are consequences for such actions. Regardless of how you feel personally toward Mr. Keaton—"

"Frankly," Jared's mom bristled, "my personal feelings are none of your business. Have you asked Mr. Keaton who it was that changed his mind?"

Mr. Wilcox frowned at the interruption. He paused a moment before replying. Finally, he replied coolly, "We have."

"And?"

Mr. Wilcox leaned forward, and Jared could see that the assistant superintendent was growing even more impatient. "And he refuses to tell us. He *says* he promised that person he wouldn't say anything." The scowl at the end of his remark telegraphed how little he thought of that promise.

Jared's mother leaned forward, too, and her eyes locked on Mr. Wilcox's. "Let me make this perfectly clear to you and everyone else at this table. I made no such request of Mr. Keaton."

"And how can we be sure of that?"

"Because I know who did," came a voice from behind them.

Everyone turned to see Ellie Brejovic standing with her father in the doorway.

CHAPTER 25

Mr. Keaton stood and went to the door. "Ellie," he said. "How did you—?"

"Papa heard it on the news," she said.

The teacher shook his head. "You don't have to do this. Really."

Ellie smiled at him. "I know," she said. Even from across the room Jared could see how blue her eyes were. Even bluer than the shirt she wore—

Jared blinked. Her shirt. Rafe wasn't the one who'd been listening in the hallway that afternoon. It was Ellie!

Mr. Brejovic spoke to the superintendent. "I am sorry to be coming here with no . . ." He paused.

"Invitation," Ellie prompted.

Mr. Brejovic smiled, his pride in his daughter evident in

his eyes. "With no invitation," he continued, "but my daughter, Illyana Brejovic, she has something to be saying about this matter. She goes to school for Mr. Keaton."

Ms. Janes rose along with Mr. Wilcox and Mr. Malavi, and she motioned for Ellie and her father to sit down. Ellie did so, but her father remained standing by the door. "Ellie is the one with the something to be saying," he explained. But Ms. Janes urged him to sit anyway, and Jared thought he detected relief in the big man's eyes when he took a seat, easing his right foot under the massive table.

"Very well," said Ms. Janes. She repeated the introductions and she and the two men took their seats again. "You have something to tell us, Ellie?" she asked.

Ellie nodded. "Mr. Keaton's in trouble because of something I asked him to do," she said.

"And what would that be?" asked Mr. Wilcox.

"I asked him to let Jared write a second test."

Jared looked at her, his mouth open. *Catching flies,* his mother used to tease him when she saw him like that. He closed his mouth, but he continued to stare at Ellie. After what he had done, lying about cheating just so Rafe and the others wouldn't know he'd spent time with her, Ellie had asked the teacher to give Jared a second chance. *I wouldn't do to my worst enemy what you did to Ellie.* Steve was right. And look what Ellie had done in return.

"And what," asked Mr. Wilcox, "made you think that you could change his mind?"

Ellie spoke clearly and firmly, and Jared recognized in her voice the same tone she used when she helped him with his math. She wasn't going to go too fast; she wanted to make sure everyone kept up. He smiled to himself as she explained, "I tutored Jared in math three or four times a week this past month. He had some real problems at the beginning, but they weren't as big as he thought they were. Mostly, he had just convinced himself he couldn't do it. But, as Mr. Keaton tells us, everyone can do math. It's just that some of us don't have enough strategies. I just helped Jared see how the strategies worked."

"Do you get paid for your tutoring?" asked Mr. Wilcox.

"It's part of the extracurricular program at our school," said Ellie. "Everybody has to take part in at least one out-of-class activity. I'm lousy at sports, so I tutor." She nodded her head toward the teacher. "You know, it was Mr. Keaton who first came up with the idea of the extracurricular requirement."

Jared was surprised to hear that. He looked at Mr. Keaton, but the teacher was looking intently at Ellie. He had the same look on his face that Ellie's dad wore as he watched his daughter speak so confidently to these adults.

Ellie continued, "I heard our principal in the hallway one day telling Mr. Keaton how glad he was that Mr. Keaton thought it up, how it's really helped a lot of kids.

It helped me. When the school year started, I hated the thought of having to do something extracurricular. I'm kind of a loner." Jared could hear her swallow before she went on. "But it helped me get used to talking to someone my age. I know that doesn't sound like much, but it's not an easy thing when you don't have friends."

Jared's eyes widened. Not once had he thought about how difficult the tutoring might have been on Ellie. Not once.

Ms. Janes leaned forward. "This is all very nice, Ellie, but I still don't understand why you felt you should ask Mr. Keaton to change his rewrite policy for Jared."

"Jared *knew* that math. It's just that he froze when he saw the test. I ought to know. I worked with him one on one for hours, and he made some terrific marks—"

"We heard about those marks," interrupted Mr. Wilcox. "Rafe Wells told us that you helped Jared cheat on his quizzes to *get* those marks."

Ellie looked down at her lap, her face crimson. Jared could feel his mother's eyes on him, along with everyone else's.

"Mr. Wilcox," said Jared, "can I say something?"

Mr. Wilcox turned to him, the anger in his eyes enough to burn holes in Jared's face. "Did you not tell Rafe that Ellie helped you cheat on your math quizzes?"

Jared nodded, and he felt his mother slump in her chair. "But I was lyin'. She didn't."

"Let me get this straight," said Mr. Wilcox. "You *lied* to make people think that Ellie helped you cheat." He turned to Ms. Janes and Mr. Malavi. "In my day, we lied to make people think we *hadn't* cheated."

Jared's face felt as red as Ellie's. "I know it sounds stupid, and it is. Real stupid. I was just embarrassed about spendin' so much time with Ellie. I thought everyone would think I was . . . you know. . . ."

"*Friends* with her?" asked Ms. Janes softly.

Jared nodded. "Yeah. Friends with her."

"And you decided you'd rather have people think you were a cheater than a friend of the girl who had helped you do so well in math," said Mr. Wilcox. He didn't even try to hide the contempt in his voice.

Ashamed, Jared looked down at the table. "A friend 'a mine told me to think how that musta made her feel."

"And did you?" demanded Mr. Wilcox.

"I been thinkin' about that a lot." Jared turned to Ellie. "I'm real sorry, Ellie. I was such a jerk."

Ms. Janes addressed everyone in the room. "It would appear that we've wasted everyone's time here today. Worse than that, however," and she looked at the teacher, "it appears we were intentionally misled in our understanding of the situation, Mr. Keaton. It's clear from our interview earlier with your principal, Mr. Rideout, and from the comments of these students, that you are indeed a teacher of great integrity. Keeping your promise not to reveal Ellie's part in your decision is an excellent example of that." She turned to Ellie. "May I ask why you didn't want anyone to know what you'd done?"

Ellie lowered her eyes. "I didn't want Jared to have to worry about his friends finding out."

Jared groaned inwardly. Despite the lousy thing he'd done to her, Ellie had still only been thinking about how he'd feel. He was ashamed of himself all over again.

"And," Ellie continued, "I didn't want him to have to lie any more about cheating. When he failed the first test so badly, it really did look like he'd been cheating on the quizzes."

"Hey," Jared said softly, "I made an eighty-eight on the rewrite."

Ellie looked at him and smiled shyly. "I *told* you you could do it, didn't I?"

CHAPTER 26

The cheers were deafening.

When the whistle blew at the half, the Cougars were up by one. The score had ping-ponged between the Cougars and the Mustangs throughout the game, and every Cougar knew he had to come out for the second half with a clear head and an eye on the outcome.

It had been a remarkable season, and Jamieson had praised each player repeatedly in the final minutes before the championship game began, but here, he'd said, was where the rubber met the road. Jared had grinned when he'd heard the coach use that line. He'd looked at the stands and saw Ron—Jared now had to remember to call him *Mr. Keaton* in school—give him a thumbs-up, while his mother waved enthusiastically beside him.

Beside the teacher sat Ellie and Su Mei Hyun. Their faces were painted in Cornwallis Middle School colours, and Su Mei was laughing at something Ellie had just said. Jared thought for a moment about how little English the girl had been able to speak when she'd first arrived from Korea back in October and how much she'd progressed once Ellie had begun to tutor her.

Su Mei and Ellie had become inseparable, always chatting and giggling over one thing or another, and Jared was hard-pressed to decide which girl had benefited more from the relationship. Of course, the line between where tutoring ended and friendship began was a blurry one. Jared knew that himself. And, as he had predicted, Su Mei's academic performance was now among the strongest in the class, but it was the change he'd seen in Ellie that pleased Jared more. Although still shy around everyone except Su Mei and Jared, Ellie had started to open up during class discussions and group work, and students had begun to recognize her wicked sense of humour and her willingness to help others. Seeing how she had helped Jared with his math, some of his classmates had gone themselves to ask her for help. Even, to Jared's amazement, Pete Johnson. That was because Rafe Wells was no longer around to lend him a hand.

Rafe had transferred out of Cornwallis Middle School the Monday following the school board meeting. His father had enrolled him in an expensive private school in the city's south end, and he'd immediately joined that school's basketball team—apparently, there was never a full roster of players since most of the kids there were more into academics than athletics. The Cougars had played Rafe's team once in an invitational tournament, and it had been pretty embarrassing. Rafe had played well but, as Coach Jamieson always told them, one person doesn't win a game. Rafe's teammates missed even the simplest passes, and their shooting wasn't much better. Frustrated, Rafe had stalked off the court at the end of the first half and wouldn't go back on. The Cougars won by forty-six points.

Rafe's dad had suffered quite an embarrassment of his own—Skylar Wells had lost his bid for mayor. He'd been shaky in the polls going into the last few weeks of the election, and the whole school-complaint fiasco had ruined whatever slim chance he had. Jared figured voters found it hard to support a candidate who gave flowery speeches but couldn't seem to get his facts straight.

And Jared and his mom ended up on television after all. Diana Barnes had been waiting for them when they came out of the meeting room, and she'd cornered them in the hallway with her camera and microphone and about a zillion watts of lights. Jared had been blinded for a moment and, caught off guard, he'd started answering the questions that people were firing at him. His comment *I wouldn't do to my worst enemy what Skylar Wells did to Mr. Keaton* received a lot of airplay and even got quoted in the newspaper, to Steve's utter delight. "You *owe* me, buddy!" he'd crowed. They'd even joked that maybe Steve's future was in speech writing.

And speaking of futures, Jared was beginning to think that his interest in marine biology might not be an impossible dream, after all. For the most part, he seemed to have gotten a handle on the math thing. Every once in a while he came up against a brick wall that he thought he'd never get over, but he found that concentrating on what he *could* do rather than getting bogged down in what he *couldn't* do helped put things into perspective. And he could always ask his friend Ellie for help when he needed it.

Now, waiting for the referee to signal the beginning of the second half, Jared glanced up at the bleachers packed with Cornwallis Middle School students, teachers, and parents. He saw Ellie turn to say something to Ron and his mom, and the two adults started to laugh. There'd been a lot of laughing when Jared told his mom that he'd thought she might be getting back with his dad. "Fool me twice, shame on me," she'd said. Jared hadn't known what she'd meant by that, but it was great to see her so happy. Of course, he'd taken some ribbing from the kids in 6K about his mom and Mr. Keaton, and the teacher now seemed to be twice as hard on him in class, but Jared thought that was probably fair. Things had a way of balancing out. You just had to give them time.

A jab to the ribs jolted him from his thoughts. "You snooze, you lose," said Steve as the whistle blew and the players made their way onto the floor.

Jared grinned. "Who said anything about losin'?" he asked, positioning himself for the tipoff.

As the referee tossed the ball into the air, Jared leaped after it and raced the roar of the crowd down the court.

ACKNOWLEDGEMENTS

As always, my sincere thanks to my editor, Lynne Missen, and the rest of the team at HarperCollins for their tireless professionalism. And thanks as well to Paul Shaffner—Middleton's own "Coach Jamieson"—for making sure I got the game right.